RICK BUTLER

TURMOIL

SHORT STORIES FROM THE OIL INDUSTRY

RICK BUTLER

TURMOIL

SHORT STORIES FROM THE OIL INDUSTRY

gatekeeper press

Columbus, Ohio

turmOIL: Short Stories from the Oil Industry

Published by Gatekeeper Press
2167 Stringtown Rd, Suite 109
Columbus, OH 43123-2989
www.GatekeeperPress.com

ISBN (paperback): 9781662900464
eISBN: 9781662900471

Library of Congress Control Number: 2020936801

Table of Contents

Preface

They say when you throw a frog into a pot of boiling water it will jump out immediately, but if you place the same frog into a pot of cool water and slowly raise the water's temperature the frog will not jump out but stay and slowly cook to death.

Dramatic changes, especially those that threaten basic survival, evoke dramatic reactions. More subtle changes will either go unnoticed or can be tolerated or accommodated through adaptation.

A repeating trend of price increases for crude oil experienced by most as increases in the price of gasoline and explained away as discontinuities of supply and demand represent the pot. The consumers of gasoline and petroleum-related products are the frogs. The difficulty in recognizing the similar situation is that this has been going on for over 80 years. Pattern recognition is always easier when related events are closer together or their existence is blatantly obvious. As time extends, or as evidence is masked, patterns become more difficult to discern.

The short stories that follow are fictional glimpses into the inner workings of the oil industry and their clandestine activities to control the market for petroleum-based products. Factual events will make the stories appear real. The intent is to help you to start forming your own questions, like: What crude oil price levels can be tolerated? And, who is really controlling the market for crude? As consumers, the questions you might ask are somewhat different: Can energy adaptation be accomplished? Will a dramatic reaction to excessive pricing be triggered? Or, like the frog from the example above, will price levels be managed in such a way to just avoid forcing adaptation or the triggering of a dramatic reaction?

The stories will fall into one of five topical areas: Economics, Industry, Corporate, Military and Government. There are many points of overlap between these areas and even more points of intersection. The points of intersection, however, are really more like points of friction despite the irony of the cause being a lubricant. Lastly, try to imagine a world where crude oil, petrochemicals, and all their derivative products never existed. What would be taking its place? And, how would all of the things we take for granted each day be provided? Know that someone, somewhere, is already thinking about both questions and how to control the raw material.

The Conversation

conversation: noun - a talk, especially an informal one, between two or more people, in which news and ideas are exchanged

It was one of those conversations you weren't supposed to overhear, but the longer it went on, the more you wanted it to continue. I was sitting in the Galleries Lounge at the Dubai airport waiting for the 2:25 a.m. British Airways flight to London when the words I heard confirmed what I already knew: oil production was being manipulated to control the global price of oil per barrel. But the conversation wasn't about managing an oil-related revenue stream; it was about something else completely. The thing the speakers didn't count on was that their conversation was being heard by me.

About 47 years ago, my friends and I watched lines form at the neighborhood Vickers gas station after a nightly news reporter made everyone aware of something called an "oil embargo." The Organization of Arab Petroleum Exporting Countries (OAPEC) proclaimed an embargo in response to the U.S. decision to resupply the Israeli military during the Yom Kippur war. This wasn't the first time that

1

natural resources would be withheld for political reasons, and nor would it be the last, but it was the first time the entire globe was simultaneously impacted by the action. That was the moment I knew I had to get involved.

I read everything I could find on oil exploration, calculating reserves, drilling, production, refining and distribution, and in the days before the Internet that meant spending a lot of time in the library. The problem with that research approach, however, was the available information tended to be mostly academic or engineering oriented. One of the more recent and best sources I stumbled across was OnePetro, the SPE (Society of Petroleum Engineers) eLibrary at Princeton University. Despite not having authentication as a Princeton user, I was able to hack my way in relatively fast. What I didn't expect to find were the unredacted and unpublished transcripts of the closed-door OAPEC sessions and the confidential memos discussing the next 100 years of crude oil production management and how to control the global economy. In order to fully understand what those transcripts meant, I also needed to understand the geo-political and religious motivations behind the production of crude oil along with the micro- and macro-economic cause-and-effect relationships associated with its exploitation.

OAPEC consisted of the Arab members of OPEC plus Egypt, Syria and Tunisia. The memos outlined the existence of a very well-structured organization with multiple functions centered on a common goal; namely, to make sure all decisions around oil production and pricing were tightly held without giving the appearance of being manipulated. The organization would be geographically dispersed and direct communication between its parts was strictly controlled. It was as if all parts acted independently, but much like a marionette, they were all attached to a common cross bar. In this case, however, just like a complex marionette, the cross bar had a detachable top to allow some of its parts to move independently from the main body. Armed with the transcripts, I was in a position to anticipate the movement of the main body and, with some certainty, predict the movement of its quasi-independent parts. The dilemma I now faced was what to do with this information and who, if anyone, to notify. Operating on my own I would look like a commodities savant and be able to amass a small fortune, but I would also attract a lot of unwanted attention. Guiding a petroleum mutual fund, I could hide behind armies of research analysts and predictive models set up to manage investment capital from multiple sources while outpacing the market based upon the inside information I held. Leading a multi-national oil and natural gas conglomerate, I'd have influence over a vertically integrated company covering exploration and production, refining, distribution and marketing, petrochemicals, power generation and, of course, trading. I opted for the latter.

My education and energy-related government work experience made me a shoo-in for British Petroleum's Leadership Development Program or BP-LDP. The LDP executive sponsors were impressed with my knowledge and were in disbelief of my ability to correctly predict what was going to happen next in the market. I rotated through the entire organization quickly and advanced rapidly. I spent time in upstream, midstream and downstream operations. The upstream is sometimes known as the exploration and production (E&P) sector. The midstream sector involves the transportation (by pipeline, rail, barge, oil tanker or truck), storage, and wholesale marketing of crude or refined petroleum products. The downstream sector is the refining of petroleum crude oil and the processing and purifying of raw natural gas, as well as the marketing and distribution of products derived from crude oil and natural gas. I enjoyed the day-to-day work in downstream the most, but upstream operations gave me the chance to leverage the content of the transcripts.

I had to assume other people had seen or heard of the OAPEC transcripts but many of their actions indicated otherwise. Executives and speculators operated in direct contradiction to what the transcripts indicated would take place. It was as if they intentionally sought to lose money. Only later did I learn these opposite actions were indeed intentional in order to divert attention away from what they knew. It was done in much the same way the Allied Forces in World War II made their battle decisions after breaking the Enigma machine's code. Using a statistical model of what would not make it look like the code was broken, the Allies' knowledge of the Axis' movements could be leveraged to win just enough battles to win the overall war. In this case, just enough of the wrong steps in E&P, distribution and pricing would divert unwanted attention but achieve the outcome desired.

As the Executive Vice President of Upstream Operations and heir apparent to the CEO and President, my inside knowledge and work experience were extremely valuable, but the conversation I overheard would prove to be my most valuable asset. I would have the ability to maintain the dominance of my company and simultaneously operate another fully controllable resource generating unfathomable wealth in an industry completely unrelated to oil.

It took about two more years for me to officially become CEO and president. I had been shadowing my predecessor for the last 12 months at the request of the board, extending my relationships both inside and outside the company. During that period, I was also given full, independent, operational and P&L control over one of our largest divisions, the real estate and land management company. This turned out to be very serendipitous because of the conversation. Given our business, that meant oil fields, both on the land and in the sea, refinery locations, pipeline right of ways, and a large quantity of saltwater and freshwater ports.

The conversation led me to direct our real estate and land management company to start acquiring tracts of property that were obviously not capable of producing oil. Surprisingly, no one asked why, and no one commented on the land-based purchases being so systematic or all above 50N latitude. By the time my shadow period was over, we had become the single largest landowner in Canada behind Her Majesty's government and the largest non-governmental entity landowner in Russia.

After moving into the CEO role, I redirected our drilling division to start positioning their equipment across all the recently acquired property at 100-mile intervals, aligned east to west. I told them to be prepared to drill and pump from depths of 100 feet up to 30,000 feet when they received my signal. Again, as odd as this was, no one asked why, and no one commented. That was at least until I was preparing for my first board meeting. We always report on asset utilization and placement so there was no way to hide or avoid reporting on the redirection of this many drilling teams.

The question I was now faced with was this: do I share with the board the real reason behind the land purchases and placement of drilling teams? This would mean divulging the content of the conversation. And if I did share, would they believe it? I know I didn't when I overheard it. Given the diversity and longevity of the board members, I had to trust they'd both understand and believe the story, so I decided to come clean. The key, however, would be in the way I'd frame the expenses incurred so far and the economic and competitive advantage being created for the future. Tie-ins to controlling the release and use of a natural resource would immediately resonate with this audience as would the concepts of upstream, midstream and downstream operations. The more I could put this situation into the context of what they already understood, the more certainty I'd have about gaining their support. I would just have to move the board members as quickly as possible from disbelief to acceptance, like I did when I overheard the conversation and found out the resource being discussed was the global supply of fresh water.

At What Price?
The U.S. Perspective

price: noun - the amount of money expected, required, or given in payment for something

This wasn't like the other battlefield simulation projects I had been assigned since starting work in the Center for Naval Warfare Studies, the country's oldest war-gaming facility, because it could start a battle based upon an event of my creation. I was asked to calculate the price per barrel of oil that would force the United States to seize control of the Arabian Peninsula.

The project was as much a study of economics and understanding the global reach of petroleum-based products as it was a military exercise. Fortunately, the military part of the project would be quite easy to complete. Just like positioning pieces in a chess game, the U.S. had been positioning its bases on the peninsula as far back as 1946 and maintains daily vigil in the Persian Gulf. It would be a simple extension to shift from defensive to offensive postures and to coordinate actions with a combined sea and air invasion force effectively catching the local inhabitants between the two sides of a closing vise. Military equipment that the locals had purchased regularly from the U.S. had hidden, built-in mechanisms to render them useless upon receipt of a special broadcast message from the orbiting Global Positioning System satellites once initiated by the Pentagon.

So how to determine that price per barrel? At its most basic level, the pump price of gasoline is about the closest most people get to the price of a barrel of oil. Each 42-gallon barrel of crude oil produces about 19 gallons of gasoline. The remainder of the barrel yields distillate and residual fuel oils, jet fuel and many other products. Doing a quick calculation on a $100 barrel of oil would result in a $5.26 per gallon price of gasoline if that were the only finished product. Fortunately, the other byproducts all have value and help offset the price of gasoline. Using a very basic distilling calculation, and taking the other byproducts into account, a $100 barrel of oil leads to a $3.99 per gallon price of gasoline.

Based upon average take-home pay assumptions and the average percentage of take-home pay currently attributable to transportation-related items, we determined that gasoline prices greater than $10.00 per gallon in the U.S. would be unsupportable. This translates to a $250 barrel of oil. As of today, that barrel price has not been reached. Not that it is isn't possible; it's just that the supply and demand curves haven't moved there yet.

What's interesting about this U.S. per gallon price is that its equivalent price level has been reached and exceeded in other countries despite not having a $250 barrel of oil. The reasons for this are numerous but are primarily tied to midstream and downstream operations and efficiencies, or lack thereof. This means that every country has its own breaking point or price where it needs to take action. A country's oil price sensitivity is directly correlated with its own proven reserves of crude oil, its ability to leverage or develop alternative energy sources, or to intervene in other ways (e.g., diplomatic measures, economic sanctions, or military action).

I constructed new predictive models daily, exploiting every type of simulation I could think of and even used some suggestions made to me by others. Of course, they didn't know how I was going to be using them as this project had higher than Top Secret classification and required Code Word access. The multivariate nature of the calculations and the large number of independent and dependent variables quickly forced me well beyond the capability of a laptop or desktop computer and I ended up on the air-gapped mainframe. Of all the predictive tools I used—Markovian, Stochastic and Bayesian—the best results came from Monte Carlo analysis because it gave a set of expected results that could be readily used by the president and Cabinet members in the ever-changing socio-economic and political environment that would unfold should an intervention be required.

My follow-on work was to create similar models for each of the G20 member countries so we would know their unsupportable price per gallon. Given the vast socio-economic differences of the member countries, the independent variables were quite diverse and, as a result, there was no pattern to the output. The next step was to interconnect the 20 models and that's when things got interesting.

It took me about a week of programming to set up the mathematical model and several more days to align the variables. While the basis of the independent and dependent variables was the same, the values were dramatically different and required normalization. Because of runtime concerns, I had to set breakpoints in the combined model. This allowed me an opportunity to check the progress of the calculations and was useful for diagnostic purposes. What I didn't expect to see, however, were the multiple points of pricing intersection between countries that would otherwise not be considered connected. The other surprising result was the emergence of one variable—weather—as the largest influencer of all 20 countries in reaching their unsupportable price per gallon.

Weather impacts every part of the petroleum ecosystem from exploration to distribution. It is also the only variable that none of the 20 countries can directly control. Unfortunately, it is also the variable most impacted by the production and consumption of the very thing I've been asked to model. So how could a variable be both independent and dependent? The simple answer is that it cannot. This meant I'd have to figure out which type it was. But how to isolate them? This would require shaking some cobwebs loose from my days in applied mathematics class.

I remembered a simple test where you insert the variables into the following sentence:

'<independent variable> causes a change in <dependent variable> and it isn't possible that <dependent variable> could cause a change in <independent variable>.'

If weather and pricing were the independent and dependent variables respectively in the above sentence you'd get:

> 'Weather causes a change in pricing and it isn't possible that pricing could cause a change in weather.'

Clearly, this is a correct statement. Pricing can't change the weather. But what if weather and petroleum production were the two words? The sentence would read:

'Weather causes a change in petroleum production and it isn't possible that petroleum production could cause a change in weather.'

That combination, however, is wrong. Had I just backed into a mathematical model of climate change and global warming? It would appear so, but pursuing that angle would have to wait for another time.

When I moved back to my original purpose and the underlying assumptions, I neutralized the impact of weather by decoupling it from the source locations of the oil and the oil's destination locations for consumption. After running a series of simulations, I came to the conclusion there wasn't a price per barrel of oil that would force the United States to seize control of the Arabian Peninsula. Or better said, the price point was at such a high level that other, more catastrophic events would be taking place, making the takeover of the Arabian Peninsula an afterthought.

Potential Energy,
Potential Value, Resulting Profit

potential: adjective - *having or showing the capacity to become or develop into something in the future*

My doctoral thesis in economics was finally getting some real-world traction. I had postulated a completely new way of valuing a raw material by something other than the scarcity of the raw material itself, the EV-PS Model.

A barrel of oil equivalent (BOE) is the unit measure for unused energy resources. Expressed frequently in the financial statements of energy companies, BOEs are defined by the U.S. Internal Revenue Service as 1,700 kilowatt hours or as 5.8×10^6 British Thermal Units (BTUs). The watt is a unit of power. Power is the rate at which energy is transferred or transformed. Energy transfer can be used to do work, so power is also the rate at which work is performed. The BTU is a unit of energy. It is typically used to describe the heat value (energy content) of fuels.

From a barrel of oil, 47% is refined to gasoline for use in automobiles, 23% is refined to heating oil and diesel fuel, 18% is refined to other products, which includes petrochemical feedstock such as polypropylene, 4% is refined to propane, 10% is refined to jet fuel, and 3% is refined to asphalt. (Note, this sums to over 100% because there is approximately a 5% processing gain in refining.)

Therefore, a barrel of oil (priced at $86.40/barrel) generates approximately:

- 19 gallons of gasoline
- 9 gallons of heating oil and diesel fuel
- 7 gallons of petrochemical feedstock
- 2 gallons of propane
- 4 gallons of jet fuel
- 3 gallons of asphalt

These products, when added together and priced at today's prevailing rates, equate to:

- 19 gallons of gasoline ($3.45/gallon) = $65.55
- 9 gallons of heating oil & diesel fuel ($3.89/gallon) = $35.01
- 7 gallons of petrochemical feedstock ($.735/gallon) = $5.15
- 2 gallons of propane ($3.16/gallon) = $6.32
- 4 gallons of jet fuel ($2.97/gallon) = $11.88
- 3 gallons of asphalt ($3.00/gallon for sealer) = $9.00

for a total of $132.91. That's $46.51 ($132.91 − $86.40 = $46.51) more than the price of the underlying barrel of oil. Gasoline accounts for just under 50% (49.3% to be exact) of the total value generated from a barrel of oil.

Heating oil and diesel fuel account for another 26.3% of the total. For the finished products, the Value-to-Volume ratio is 6.1% and 5.9% positive for gasoline and heating oil/ diesel fuel, respectively. The best part of this whole equation, however, is the least obvious. Two of these three products are the most sensitive to predictable seasonal events. Gasoline demand increases in the summer and around holidays where driving is a primary mode of transportation. Cold weather in the fall and winter increases the demand for heating oil. This allows their already high value-to-volume ratios to be further exploited in the absence of an increase in the price per barrel of oil and, any increase in the price per barrel of oil can be immediately passed through, and further uplifted, to the consumer.

Projecting the price per gallon of gasoline across a range of prices per barrel of crude oil nets the following graph:

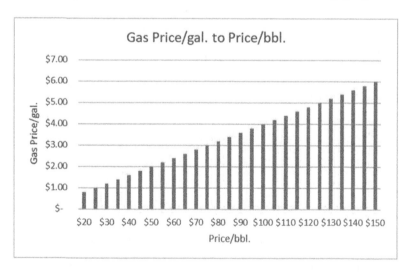

My new way of valuing a raw material was based on the economic value (EV) it creates and, because of that, also had to factor in the price sensitivity (PS) to its byproducts. In the case of crude oil, the evaluation was fairly straightforward:

Byproduct	Economic Value	Price Sensitivity
Gasoline	High	Medium
Heating oil	Low	Low
Diesel fuel	Medium	Medium
Petrochemical stock	Low	High
Propane	High	Medium
Jet fuel	Medium	Low
Asphalt	Low	Low

Whenever I would explain my evaluation approach to people, I always had to start by saying that EV is not the same as price. EV is about what the byproduct enables or contributes to. For PS, if a higher price curtails consumption, then its PS is considered high; if the consumption is not impacted by price, its PS is considered low.

The more byproducts a raw material has, the better chance for the raw material to have a high price. The higher EV of a raw material's byproducts, the better chance for the raw material to have a high price. Raw materials that are mined and refined to be another version of themselves, like gold or diamonds, do not fit this model. Their EV is based upon the actual, or perceived, scarcity of the raw material itself. In these cases, PS does not come into play at all.

The first real-world application of my valuation model, however, occurred in a space that I would have never expected: human resources or HR. Here, the raw material is an employee. The byproducts are the various roles they can play or tasks they perform. The higher the EV of the role or task, the more pay an individual could command.

If many people could fill this role or perform these tasks, the PS would be low.

As this methodology spread throughout the HR profession, it disrupted the entire process of setting target pay ranges and valuing jobs. It also upended the entire third-party salary survey industry and the way jobs were matched to the market and to other companies. And it also made me a target. I was sought out to be a guest speaker at HR conferences across the U.S. Companies asked me to consult with them on how to determine the EV of their roles and tasks. But because my work fit so well into the oil industry, I was hired as a consultant by an oil industry insider to extend the valuation methodology as an assessment and selection tool of the various channels available to distribute the byproducts of crude oil.

In the case of gasoline, the end point of the distribution channel is the gas station. By applying my valuation model to gas stations, we determined a location's EV mostly had to do with the proximity of other gas stations as well as the socio-economic status of the physical location. I'm sure we've all noticed that a given brand's gasoline price varies between neighborhoods, or from one side of the city to the other. Now you know who to blame for that!

The use of alternative distribution channels for gasoline, or the so-called private label brands, where a station is not affiliated with one of the name-brand oil companies, represents a discounted route to market for excess capacity and/or a slightly lower quality product. The energy value of gasoline sold in this way is identical to its name-brand counterpart because it is made by them; it just doesn't receive the same promotion or may have fewer additives. The per gallon pricing here is also going to be lower. Now you know who you can thank for that!

Armed with an understanding of Economic Value and Price Sensitivity, valuation assessments could be made at any point of any process but more importantly a stepwise application could also identify those items that reduced or lost value along the way. This meant the stranglehold oil companies had on basically everything could be tightened or relaxed in uncountable and invisible ways because of my model. Unlike the positive outcome enabled by John Nash's Equilibrium Model that led to new ways of valuing and bidding on wireless spectrum, my EV-PS model enabled both positive and negative outcomes depending upon who was using it.

As my consulting project came to an end, the real reason for my hiring become evident; it was to help the oil companies manage their profitability and exploit the consumer. Like most academics, I wasn't comfortable with my original work being used in unintended or harmful ways; it was supposed to be an optimization tool that benefitted everyone. Unfortunately, at this point, there wasn't anything I could do about it. Or was there?

To counteract what the oil industry was about to do with my model, I was going to need a platform with global reach and the financial backing to have an impact. Since I could predict their application and use cases faster than their ability to leverage the model's results, I would be able to put events in motion that, on the surface, seemed natural but were entirely fabricated. The four forces to be leveraged were technology, politics, economics and consumer sentiment. My connections in, and backing from, the electric vehicle and solar industries would be able to time the release of their new products to demonstrate alternatives to oil-based energy products. Politically, by virtue of my work advising Congress, the progress of new legislation and bills that were pro-environment or anti-drilling would be sped up or slowed down. Trade agreements, contacts I had at the International Monetary Fund, and Federal Reserve actions would allow the economy to flex up or down to offset manipulative industry actions. Consumer sentiment would be handled via social media, advertising and some well-placed news stories. I was about to become the poster child thorn in the side of the oil industry. My life would no longer be my own.

The Mathematics of Petroleum

mathematics: noun - the abstract science of number, quantity, and space

Math is all around us. Those words were no more evident than the first day I walked into Shell Oil's headquarters building on Main Street in downtown Houston, Texas. What I didn't realize was that everything I experienced upon arriving in Houston was going to be a test of my observational and mathematical skills.

I stayed at the Hyatt Regency hotel about three and a half blocks away from the Shell building the night before my onsite visit. It was your typical Hyatt with the completely open interior atrium reaching some 30 stories in height; however, the building was not square and was more triangular in shape, forcing all its guest rooms to be somewhat angular.

After signing in with what looked like about 75 other new hires, we proceeded to a meeting room for orientation. The presentation lasted all morning and concluded with lunch. During the morning break and lunch, I had the opportunity to network with the other new hires, comparing notes on schools, degrees and the like. We also talked about the jobs we were hired to perform and departments we were going to join. Everyone that day had either a Master's or Doctorate degree in Chemical or Petroleum Engineering except for me. Mine was in Applied Mathematics.

After lunch, supervisors for all of the attendees showed up to escort their new hires back to their respective offices. All that is, except mine. No one came to get me. I was left in the meeting room all alone. Even the morning's presentation staff and food service people had exited. Unsure of what to do next, I pulled out my laptop to review my Offer Letter and Welcome package for my supervisor's name. Before I could find the name, however, the door opened, and a man walked in wearing a white lab coat over what appeared to be a three-piece suit without the jacket. No pleasantries were exchanged; all I heard was "come with me."

We boarded what looked to be a private express elevator and ascended the Shell tower to the top floor. Once the elevator door opened, I could see about 15 more people dressed identically to my escort. They each had anywhere from six to twelve flat-screen monitors in front of them, some with dynamic charts and graphs, others with what looked like live news feeds and streaming video from oil fields all around the world. I was pointed to a vacant desk with monitors similar to the other people, told to sit down and not to talk to anyone.

On the opposite wall, I could make out doors to what appeared to be four private offices. Three were labeled Upstream, Midstream and Downstream. The fourth was labeled CEO. In front of each door were three people. I assumed they were the Executive Assistants, Chief of

Staffs and bodyguards of the individuals in the offices. Just as I sat down, my center and largest monitor came to life with a full-screen message that I will never forget:

You are now one of the most important people in the worldwide petroleum business.

The work and conversations that take place here may not leave this room.

<Click to Acknowledge & Accept>

This struck me as strange being educated as a Mathematician and not in Petroleum Engineering but nonetheless, I dutifully clicked in the appropriate spot and with that, all of my monitors came to life. I also had to lean in for a mandatory retina and fingerprint scan that would be used for subsequent logins every time I left and returned to my workstation.

Over the next several days, my work assignments and the data I had access to provided me with the reasons behind this level of security. It would also confirm the statement about me now being "one of the most important people in the worldwide petroleum business." As an example, in one project I was asked to create a single-day, artificial crude oil price arbitrage situation, and was supposed to identify and track the buyers and sellers taking advantage of it. The next day, we imposed actual supply and price penalties on those same buyers and sellers. Another project was to simulate the pricing impact of a sudden and prolonged loss of crude production capacity from a group of on- and off-shore wells. This scenario would come into play as the result of either a hurricane or industrial accident.

Over the next three months, I was assigned an assortment of projects that were all mathematical in nature with no apparent connections to the oil industry. Given the company I was working for, that struck me as strange, but I complied by delivering my work products and predictive models on time. Occasionally, I'd get the chance to compare notes with the other 15 people like me in the room and it turned out we all had been tasked with doing various mathematical projects. None of us could figure out the purpose of these models nor could we connect the dots between them. That was, at least, until the meeting.

It showed up as a nondescript, day-long Outlook meeting invite with a To: list that included 21 people; the 16 of us, the heads of Upstream, Midstream and Downstream, the CEO, and one name I didn't recognize.

Most everyone arrived in the conference room at the same time I did and all were immediately recognizable except for the lady at the front of the room. Once we all settled down, the unknown lady stood up and without introduction projected a slide showing individual thumbnails of everyone's models grouped alphabetically by author. She asked if we all recognized our various work products, to which everyone nodded affirmatively. She then advanced the slide and all of the thumbnails were realigned from left to right and top to bottom in a way that showed the output of one model becoming the input to another model. Upon advancing the slide one more time, only the first model and input along with the last model and output were showing. It was then that the power of the individual models working in conjunction with each other became evident and the reality of being one of the most important people in the worldwide petroleum industry made sense. I wondered if anyone else in the room felt that way, but then, how could they? The input and output models that remained on the screen were mine.

I tried to think back to what the requested scenarios were that led me to create these two models and in the moment I couldn't remember. Only after the meeting adjourned and I was asked to stay behind in the conference room did things come into focus. The area of interest was my pricing model that predicted the impact of a sudden and prolonged loss of crude production capacity. It turned out we needed to increase profitability and were going to do so by intentionally turning off production capacity to buoy prices. This would be done under the guise of being hacked, or industrial espionage. The only difference here was we were going to be doing it to ourselves.

The Petroleum Club

club: noun - *an association or organization dedicated to a particular interest or activity*

This was a membership club unlike any others. Founded to be an exclusive, handsome club of and for men of the oil industry, it rapidly became a key location to conduct business and seal deals with a handshake. The popular television series *Dallas* held J.R.'s memorial service at the fictionalized Dallas Petroleum Club.

There are thirteen real Petroleum Clubs in the United States and another two sharing the name in Canada. Their locations are where you'd expect: Anchorage, Long Beach, Bakersfield, Wichita, Lafayette, Morgan City, Shreveport, Billings, Oklahoma City, Fort Worth, Midland, San Antonio, Casper, Calgary and Edmonton. Each club has one or more connections to locations with upstream, midstream or downstream operations.

Operating in plain sight, its members make up the Western Hemisphere's version of OAPEC (now OPEC). They formed the secret organization called S-O-P, the State Oil Producers. The idea for S-O-P had been kicking around for a while and was more formally floated in 1988 by then-Governor of Louisiana, Buddy Roemer. And while the idea never found public traction, representatives from the contiguous states came together to form SOP. The beauty of saying the name as letters, S-O-P, was that it could be referred to openly as it was also the same acronym for Standard Operating Procedure. So, when someone would say they were following S-O-P, there were always two interpretations: one for the members and one for everyone else.

I remember the first time I looked at one of my company's geo-seismic maps designated 43-BZD and commented about the significant change of density in the rock strata indicating an extraordinarily large, and unlabeled, deposit of oil. One of my coworkers said to me, "We don't talk about that .... It's SOP." I asked, "What part? Not labeling it or not talking about it?" The answer was "Both." Since I was new to the company, I wrote it off as something I'd probably learn about later. About two weeks after that, I was in another meeting looking at another geo-seismic map designated 50-AXT and made the same observation. The reaction was identical, "We don't talk about that .... It's SOP." This was more than coincidental; it was a programmed response. That was also the last time I saw any of the maps, at least up close.

Since my day job didn't require the maps, it took me several months before it even occurred to me that I hadn't seen one in a while. I'd occasionally hear people talking about the maps in the cafeteria and knew of other workers that regularly used them. One day as I was walking between the various conference rooms on the 32nd floor, I noticed several doors with those 3x4 phone-style matrix keypads built into them. While that in and of itself wasn't all that unusual, it was what I did see that was. In place of the normal hyphenated five-digit numeric nameplate was the label SOP. At my next meeting I asked someone about the doors. Their response was, "We don't talk about that .... It's SOP." I instantly flashed back to the two other times I heard that phrase, and it made my head snap back slightly. There was obviously something else going on here and I knew I had to get into one of those rooms.

I continued to do my job and had success moving through the organization, building trust along the way and expanding the scope of my responsibilities. Then one day I got invited to lunch by my organization's Senior Vice President. We were going to the local Petroleum Club! As we entered the building's elevator, I noticed the 3×4 keypad on the floor selection panel and watched as the access code was typed in: 1, 2, 6, 7. The doors closed; the elevator rose to the 39th floor, and when the doors opened again we were in the dark wood-paneled lobby of the club. The facility was well-appointed, and the lunch meal was slightly upscale, but it was what I learned during the conversation that made the event totally worthwhile. We spoke about proved reserves, proved and probable reserves, and proved, probable and possible reserves. In the petroleum business, these are also known as 1P, 2P and 3P respectively. The market value of each is directly proportional to the degree of confidence in the size of the reserve. The conversation then shifted to more subdued tones as I listened to an explanation of where the real value resided, namely reserves that are proved but hidden. I instantly knew this had to be those areas of density change in the rock strata I previously saw indicating extraordinarily large and unlabeled deposits of oil.

Once back at my desk, I kept my head down and completed my work for the day. Since I had been out for several hours, however, I ended up being the last one in the office when I finished my work. Rather than walk out right away, I went back up to the 32nd floor. As I stood outside one of the doors labeled SOP, I glanced at the 3x4 keypad and wondered, could it be that simple? I typed in 1, 2, 6, 7. The lock clicked, and the door opened. As I walked through the door, the overhead lights came on automatically and I found myself in a map room.

The map room's walls were lined with stacked Sandusky Lee 5-drawer flat file cabinets. Each drawer had a two-digit number on it followed by three letters. The numbers ran from 01 to 50; the three letters looked to run from AAA to ZZZ. There was also a large light table in the middle of the room with two geo-seismic maps: 02-AAZ and 11-FAM. The word "spruce" was written on the edge of 02-AAZ. The 11-FAM map had what looked like a series of eight irregularly shaped circles of increasing size on a diagonal from top-left to bottom-right. I moved over to one of the file cabinets and opened the top drawer: 36-ABX. The first sheet was a translucent vellum topographical map of something that looked like a panhandle as best as I could tell. The second sheet was a geo-seismic map like the ones I had previously seen. This one was also designated 36-ABX. The geo-seismic map had no landmarks or other identifying details on it but there were unique alignment or orientation marks on each corner resembling QR codes. When used in conjunction with, and aligned under its associated vellum topographical map, specific landmarks and physical locations could be identified. One document, however, was worthless without the other, much like a lock without its key. With both documents, those density changes and unlabeled deposits of oil I previously saw could all be located.

As I looked up from the maps and started to take in the enormity of everything around me, I started to get very nervous and knew it was time to leave. I carefully placed the two 36-ABX maps back into their drawer and moved to exit the room. Of course, the door I came in had closed behind me and to get out I had to enter another code number. I again typed in 1, 2, 6, 7 but this time the lock didn't click. So now what? Since everything up to this point seemed to follow some apparent pattern, I took a deep breath and started to think. Because it was so simple to enter, it had to be simple to exit. I typed in the code number in reverse order: 7, 6, 2, 1. The lock clicked, and the door opened. As I walked out the door, the lights turned off, and I was now free to go contemplate what I had just discovered. So, why the secrecy and why the security? Well, it turned out the security was easy if you just thought about it. You see, 1267 is the Hazardous Material Code for petroleum crude oil. The secrecy, however, was a much more complex topic.

On the company-provided bus ride home, I started to wonder if the numbers on the maps and drawers had any significance or if they were simply set up for convenience of filing. I pulled out my tablet and in OneNote typed a column with the numbers and letters I had seen. I then wrote down the other details I recalled seeing on each of the maps:

02-AAZ Spruce
11-FAM Eight dots of increasing size on a diagonal from top-left to bottom-right

36-ABX Panhandle

43-BZD

50-AXT

Other than the format of the numbers, there didn't seem to be an obvious pattern. The only thing I knew for certain was their connection to specific places. I probably needed a few more data points to figure this out which meant I needed to go back into one of the map rooms.

As I closed my tablet, I flashed back to the lunchtime conversation regarding the three standard types of oil reserves plus the fourth "hidden" one. It reminded me of a thought matrix that former Secretary of Defense Donald Rumsfeld often used. He described it as follows, "[T]here are known knowns; there are things we know we know. We also know there are known unknowns; that is to say we know there are some things we do not know. But there are also unknown unknowns—the ones we don't know we don't know."

This type of classification system is common in project management and strategic planning circles, and is also used at NASA, but not a common approach used in the petroleum industry. If it were, 1P would be the "known knowns," 2P would be the "known unknowns." By extension, 3P would be the "unknown knowns" which leaves the fourth "hidden" reserve as the "unknown unknowns," except someone does know about it: SOP.

The next day back in the office, I kept thinking about the filing numbers. I used my laptop and connection to the company network to start querying various tools and databases with the combinations of numbers, letters and miscellaneous information I had assembled. I was getting nowhere until I split up the two-digit number from the three letters. The combination of 02 and Spruce led to Alaska. 36 and Panhandle led to Oklahoma. By listing the states in alphabetical order and assigning them with a numeric position I was able to conclude 11 was Hawaii, 43 was Texas and 50 was Wyoming. The eight dots of increasing size on the diagonal from top-left to bottom-right associated with 11-FAM now made sense as they were the eight Hawaiian Islands. But what did the three letters mean? That would be the next puzzle to solve.

I tried multiple ways of using the letters as abbreviations for words, positional coordinates in a three-dimensional space, relating them to their associated state number, and even tried to see if they made sense as international airport codes in the IATA list. Nothing made sense or connected. I even resorted to the "what3words" app on my phone to see if by some coincidence the letters lined up there. They didn't. Then I remembered from orientation that the company uses the size of an oil field, the quality/type of oil and the depth/degree of extraction difficulty as a way to assess its reserves. Could the three letters map to those three dimensions? So, I started laying out the table. When I did everything became clear.

	Size	Quality	Difficulty
A	Largest	Best	Easiest
.			
M	Medium	Average	Medium
.			
Z	Smallest	Worst	Hardest

Linking that back to all of the maps I had seen netted the following:

02-AAZ Alaska, largest deposit of the best quality but the hardest to extract

11-FAM Hawaii, reasonable size of the best quality with medium difficulty to extract

36-ABX Oklahoma, largest deposit of very high quality but hard to extract

43-BZD Texas, very large deposit of worst quality but easy to extract

50-AXT Wyoming, largest deposit of very low quality and somewhat hard to extract

Now, what to do with all of this knowledge? I couldn't tell anyone at the office, and I couldn't go public with it, so was there a way to use it to be more effective at my job or should I use it for my own advantage? This is what would consume all of my waking thoughts for the rest of my professional life.

Managing the Profit Pipeline

profit: noun - a financial gain, especially the difference between the amount earned and the amount spent in buying, operating, or producing something

Why do gas pump prices go up immediately when the price per barrel of oil goes up? Gasoline in transit from the refinery to the consumer was extracted as oil at the well head and sold at a different price per barrel than today's spot rate for oil. Gasoline already in the storage tanks at gas stations or distribution centers was extracted as oil at the well head even earlier. If the well head was directly connected to the gas station or distribution center, one could understand this price transference as there would be no way to discern today's product from yesterday's extraction, but that is not the case.

I'm reminded of my days living in Brazil in the mid-1990s during the era of hyper-inflation. Prices for everything went up every day. Purchasing hard goods was the only way to lock in value. Many items, including some that would surprise you, could be purchased on installment plans.

Individuals who were paid cash on a daily basis would completely spend that day's earnings on 50-pound bags of rice, beans or long-life milk. Workers paid weekly or biweekly moved and managed their money on a daily basis from long-term (weekly or monthly) interest-bearing or inflation-adjusted accounts to short-term (daily) accounts based on that day's spending needs.

When I tried to explain this to someone back in the U.S., the only way I found to explain hyper-inflation was to use a gas pump analogy. As you're pumping gas, the cost of your purchase increases based upon the amount of gas being put into your gas tank and the posted "fixed" price per gallon of the octane grade you select. In a hyper-inflation environment, the posted price per gallon would also be increasing with each gallon you pump, meaning the next gallon pumped costs more than the previous one. So, what's the connection to price transference? The connection is the need to understand how fast the channel does, or can, react.

My job is to define, monitor and control this channel. I created this position for myself much to the chagrin of my colleagues and, more so, my manager. I was educated, trained and hired to be an economist, so the first thing I had to do was to convince everyone of my value and that petroleum is an economic force and not just a source of energy. As an economic force, its power flows to and from those who control it and has an immediate and instantaneous impact on everyone and everything else. Now here's a connection that I had never made before. The noun "economics" is defined as the branch of knowledge concerned with the production, consumption, and transfer of wealth. Although never mentioned in any of my economics classes, there is no better embodiment of economics than the oil industry. In fact, the concepts of wealth production, transfer and consumption are eerily the same. Price transference, or channel efficiency, was what I was asked to assess and to optimize. Since I had a good grasp of financial concepts but no understanding of the oil industry, I figured I'd use pure economics to guide my work. I started with microeconomics and a simple model of supply and demand viewed from the opposing sides of oil consumer and oil supplier. While the channel would come into play here as a physical delivery mechanism, its efficiency wouldn't need to be factored into the mix.

On the demand side, the consumer profile was as you'd expect. I put in as many of the consumption influencers I could think of, including some at the fringe, like intentionally driving gas guzzlers and high-performance vehicles. What I found were three distinct consumption factors: work, leisure and weather.

On the supply side, I had to rely upon third-party research and industry experts to understand the demand influences. In this space, supply also boiled down to three factors: availability of the raw material, production capacity and market conditions. The latter, market conditions, included everything from the global political and trade environment to exchange rates.

As I created my econometric model, the first task was to see which of the factors had the biggest impact. I isolated supply from demand and then worked to assemble a single variable to account for market conditions since it represented multiple things. The blending of factors is not an ideal approach but if the items are somewhat homogenous, it works. I was fortunate that politics, trade and exchange rates all moved up and down in a similar fashion and about at the same time with one item only slightly lagging the others. Having a total of six variables, three on each side of the supply and demand equation, meant there were over 46,000 combinations to look at. In the days before computers, that would have been a lot of manual calculations, so we would have spent most of our upfront time eliminating unlikely combinations based upon the most likely set of assumptions. Today, the quantity of calculations is not a limitation, but you still need to start with the right set of assumptions.

One demand factor, weather, exerted control over the other two, work and leisure, and those two moved in somewhat opposite directions with each other. Work and leisure obviously have no control over weather. One supply factor, market conditions, exerted some control over production capacity and it could be argued that production capacity exerted some control over market conditions, but neither had control over the availability of raw materials.

Since I had been asked to optimize price transference, and ultimately profitability, my objective was to create as tight a connection as possible between the price at the pump and those factors capable of impacting price. The connection would not be entirely physical; it would also be psychological. Being part of the supply side of the model, manipulating information about the availability of raw materials and production capacity would be my primary tool. Manipulating the conversion of raw materials to finished products would be my secondary tool. Using both in conjunction with each other meant I had to shorten either the perceived or actual time from the well head to the gas pump and draw down the amount of product in storage tanks and reduce the amounts in transit. By slowing delivery, excess inventory would naturally decrease. Replacing that inventory would require the use of both raw and refined materials that reflect more current pricing than the materials being replaced.

In order to drive this point home with my colleagues, I created a graphical representation showing the inverse relationship between product delivery and stored inventory, the price trend of finished goods, and their connections to an already profitable value chain. The key was to be in "The Zone".

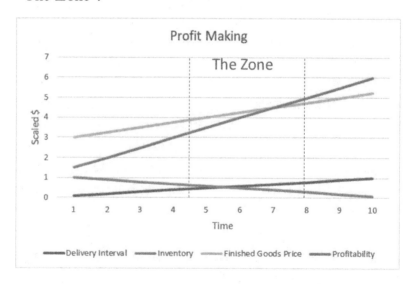

Finding and managing the crossover points between having too little inventory and the speed at which new product could be delivered would be a primary way to increase profitability. My identification of these crossover points, and understanding the sensitivity between them, satisfied the task I was asked to do and gave validity to the job I created. Only time would tell if my colleagues and my manager would change their mind about me.

Engines that Run on Water

engine: noun - a machine with moving parts that converts power into motion

I remember a story my late uncle would tell about an exposition he went to where an inventor was demonstrating an automobile engine running on water. The most interesting part of the story to me, however, was when he said the demonstration made the local news that week but then as quickly at the story broke, the engine, the story and the inventor disappeared. Rumors developed that the oil companies made sure that the engine, the story and the inventor would never see the light of day again. So far that has been the case.

As I started to do my research on the exposition, I found an opening session's version of the show's brochure listing the inventor's booth along with an explanation of what was being demonstrated. Another copy of the show's brochure published later in the week, however, did not include the booth. The booth numbers had a gap in the sequence where it was obvious a booth had been deleted. The map of the expo floor showed a blank spot where the booth had previously been placed. What no one counted on was the fact that my uncle had taken an 8mm movie walking towards and away from the demonstration and booth itself. I now have the film. It is the equivalent of the Zapruder film from the Kennedy assassination except this film showed information that was about to be killed.

The film canister was nondescript except for the usual dents and scratches that the old gray and brown metallic film holders tended to pick up. The adhesive label had the handwritten notation, Future Tech Expo '52 and the numbers 12391013. I ran across the film canister while going through my uncle's personal effects looking for family memorabilia.

When I got back home with the film, it took me a few hours to locate our old Revere De-Luxe 8mm Model 85 projector that hadn't seen the light of day for thirty-plus years. I was hoping the projector's bulb would light and that the spindles would turn. They did.

There was no sound recorded on the film. The only noise in the room was the whirring of the projector's cooling fan and the clicking of the film's sprockets progressing through the projector's claw film guides that steady the film. As I watched the short film, I could clearly see the booth, the engine and the inventor, and signage explaining the science behind the demonstration. This booth was in the middle of an aisle with what looked to be about twenty other booths.

As the film spun off its reel and progressed through the rest of the projector, I noticed what seemed to be some letters and a series of numbers printed on a strip of narrow, light blue adhesive tape placed around the innermost part of the film's original spool. The tape was not visible on the reel when the film was wrapped around it. Before rewinding the film back onto its original spool, I copied down the numbers from the tape: FNBSTL39066232.

After I placed the rewound film back into its metal canister, I started to wonder what the letters and numbers could mean. Since they didn't look like anything else I had seen before, I went to the most logical place to see what I could find out, my internet search engine. Loading in the whole string netted the response: Your search - FNBSTL39066232 - did not match any documents. Loading in the letters only returned: Central Bank. It turns out Central Bank is the successor organization to the First National Bank in St. Louis (FNBSTL). That then must mean the numbers are either an account number or a box number. Unfortunately, since the original bank is no longer in existence, the ability to back-track the number would be difficult.

Nonetheless, I went to one of the Central Bank branch locations the next day to see what I could find out. After being assigned to one of the personal bankers, I explained I had either an old account or box number from the First National Bank in St. Louis and was trying to find out if the account or box was still valid. As she typed in the information and the results appeared on her screen, her posture and demeanor changed significantly. She asked that we move out of the open cubicles on the main floor of the branch and into one of the private offices. Once inside the office, she re-entered the information I had previously provided and then asked me if I had the eight-digit password on the account. That struck me as odd, but it was more frustrating because I didn't have any other numbers to provide. That was at least until I remembered the label from the film canister and the number, 12391013. Once I provided this number and the personal banker entered it into her terminal, she very formally asked, "How may I assist you?"

Not knowing what to say, or what she was looking at, I asked her for a complete statement of the account from inception. She looked at me somewhat incredulously and said the account started back in 1952 with a very large deposit and showed equally large quarterly deposits from an offshore source every year since but they had stopped in March 2016, the month and year my uncle passed away. The last one was from First Gulf Bank. There were also large, annual wire transfer withdrawals to banks and stockbrokers in Chicago, New York, multiple cities throughout California, and even to banks in Winnipeg, Canada. Those ended at the end of 2015. She then told me the Central Bank account in St. Louis still had a very large positive balance and asked me what else she could help me with. I said there was nothing else I needed at this point and thanked her for her help and information. She walked me out through a nondescript rear door of the bank branch that opened into a courtyard of shops and restaurants behind the bank.

As I walked into the courtyard, a flood of memories came to me about all of the conversations, experiences and lessons I had with my uncle that involved money. One of my favorite recollections was on the day before Christmas Eve in 1966. He had just arrived at my grandparents' house and saw they didn't have a Christmas tree. I happened to be there visiting with my mother and he asked me to go shopping with him. There was nothing special about how my uncle dressed or the car he drove, but the way he carried himself changed when we walked into the store. He asked a salesperson to stay by our side and we immediately went to the Trim-A-Tree section of the store. As we moved through the department, he pointed at things on both sides of the aisle and the salesperson asked his counterparts to pull them down. At one point, we stopped at an elevated display of fully decorated trees and he pointed at one of them. The salesperson said, "Those aren't for sale," to which my uncle said, "If it is in the store, it's for sale." By this time one of the store managers had also started to follow us around. It was at this point the manager intervened and asked a surprising question, "Would you like it with or without the decorations?" My uncle's answer was predictable: "With the decorations, of course." He asked me to stay and supervise the packing process while he, the manager and the salesperson who had been helping us walked over to the cash register to pay. As we were packing up the car, I asked him how much he spent and all he did was grin and said, "You don't need to know and it's none of your business."

My second memory regarding money occurred when I spent the summer of 1971 with him in the southern California desert. On one evening he said he was going to teach me about the stock market and that we'd need to get an early start the next day. We got up about 5:30 a.m. and after the usual half grapefruit and slice of coffee cake, we got in the car and drove downtown to the office of Merrill-Lynch. Even though it was about 6:15 a.m. the place was already open and people were actively moving around, on the phones and talking with other customers who had arrived before us. I wasn't quite sure what to expect but did notice this large, illuminated sign high on the wall. All of the desks faced this sign as it flashed a countdown timer showing 13 minutes.

As I watched the timer run down to zero, the display changed to Market Open and immediately a stream of capital letters followed by a one-, two- or three-digit number appeared, each followed by an 's' along with another one-, two- or three-digit number followed by fractions that were in multiples of 1/8. My uncle sat down with me and explained the letters were symbols representing the stocks of companies, the numbers with the 's' represented quantities of shares in multiples of 100 and the other numbers were the price per share. He then stepped away to talk with one of the people sitting at the desks and when he came back, he told me to watch for several pairs of letters and to pay attention to the numbers that followed them with the 's' and the numbers with the fractions. He explained these were "buy" orders he had just placed. I thought it was very cool that something he just did in the office where we were would appear on the sign and that it represented a transaction made at his request in New York. He said that most people focus on when to buy a stock but it is more important to know when to sell it. He also said that if you couldn't explain what a company does in 25 words or less you have no business in owning its stock. I didn't think much about it at the time, but in retrospect when I reflect back on the symbols, they were all oil companies. When I did the math in my head, I realized the values involved were in the tens of thousands of dollars each. While the numbers impressed me at the time, the guidance on buying and selling stocks left the biggest impression.

My third memory came from when he and my mother visited me while I was living and working in Brazil in 1994.

I shared with him the details of my stock portfolio, how I tracked it, and how I used his teachings to buy and sell stocks. I think that both surprised and pleased him. He then told me to purchase two stocks because one of them would be splitting within the next 12 months and that the other would be doubling in value within 24 months. I asked him how he knew but he said nothing. I followed his guidance and everything happened just as he said it would. Ten years later, when I was back at his house in the desert, I asked him how he knew what was going to happen with those two stocks and he pointed to a stack of annual reports on his coffee table that he called his "leisure reading." As I flipped through the reports, they all shared a common theme, petrochemicals, and he had highlighted several financial tables and footnotes in each.

No one in the family could ever figure out how my uncle had amassed the monies he had. Certainly, he was successful in the land development and property management business in southern California but the path to that career in the early 1970s was incongruous with his work as a hospital administrator in the 1960s. He didn't really spend money flamboyantly, or on anything extraneous for that matter. He constantly shopped for deals and bargains, went to flea and farmer's markets regularly, only purchased things when they were on sale, and lived well below his likely means. It was only when I started to piece together the date of his death, with the timing of the last deposit into the FNBSTL account, and the date of the last wire transfer withdrawal, did the pieces start to fall into place. This 8mm film must somehow factor in.

Could this film have been the source of his wealth? Was someone paying him not to share or expose the content of the film? Beyond capturing the image of the missing booth, the engine and the inventor, did the film record something or someone else? I'm afraid we'll never know these answers for sure as the what and the who in the film have long since disappeared. But who knew to stop the quarterly deposits upon my uncle's death? And more importantly, did they know I now had the film? Maybe I shouldn't have gone to the bank.

About a week later, as I was accessing my checking account from my phone, I noticed the balance was much larger than I recall it being, or had ever been for that matter. My usual four- or five-digit balance was six very large digits. When I looked at the account detail screen, I saw a large deposit that took place the day after I visited Central Bank. The source was an offshore bank. I immediately contacted my bank to question the deposit as an error so they backtracked the wire transfer to its source and validated its accuracy. The bank told me the deposit was mine to keep.

To say I was dumbfounded would be an understatement. What had I stepped into? What had I started? Who knew I had asked questions about the account and how did they find out? The bank, or more specifically someone at the bank, must have been involved. If they were involved, then they must think I now have the film. From this point I started to be much more aware of my surroundings and was continuously looking for signs of being followed or having my personal spaces disrupted. There were no signs of either. I maintained my usual daily routine and my surroundings continued to be stable. I also intentionally avoided spending any of the money that was wired into my account, but the fact that it was there, and I didn't know why, just kept eating at me.

The only thing I had to go on was the somewhat cryptic wire information in my bank's mobile app All Transactions screen:

WIRE TYPE:WIRE IN DATE: 190228 TIME:1522 ET TRN:1030042009645223 SEQ:20190228002299966/ 025123 ORIG:UAE (NBAD) ACCT ID:85930772 SND BK: FIRST ABU DHABI BANK ID:XXXXXX099 PMT DET:00006504 83015 SCH REF(Y 1 00 97124996599)

It would be nearly impossible to chase down any information from the U.S., so if I wanted to find out more, I was going to have to schedule a trip to the United Arab Emirates. Going there would be risky, however, and not because of the location but because of the proximity to the source of payouts. Interestingly, if I had known about all of this fifteen years earlier, I could have used one of my work trips as cover to do my research. It turned out I was in Abu Dhabi and Dubai just before my last visit to my uncle's house. As I think about it now, when I told him and my mother about the trip and shared the pictures, he seemed particularly interested in the places I went and the businesses I saw, almost to the point of looking for something specific. He even read with interest the newspaper I had brought back and studied the city map with a magnifying glass.

If I did go to the UAE, I knew I would require a local escort and liaison to gain access to the locations and people that could possibly help me, but I also needed to be very careful this time. It was easy to find a flight to Abu Dhabi so I went ahead and booked the flight from SFO to AUH, but finding the right person to escort me in country was going to be the trick. From my 2004 trip, I still had a former work contact in Abu Dhabi that might fit the bill of what I was looking for, but they also knew the names of several well-connected people that could as well.

During the 64 years between the 1952 Future Tech Expo and my uncle's passing in 2016, I know he never traveled to the Middle East despite being a world traveler. He literally went everywhere else but seemed to consciously avoid the Gulf, almost to the point of sending a message. I started to wonder if this was his last lesson to me, another way of saying, "You don't need to know and it's none of your business." With that realization, I cancelled my Etihad Airways reservation.

Additives

additive: noun - a substance added to something in small quantities to improve or preserve it

Automobiles need gasoline to run. Oil companies need automobiles to sell their product. More miles per gallon means less gasoline is needed. More additives mean more processing expense, the use of additional raw materials and the ability to charge more.

Being part of downstream operations, I was asked to research this symbiotic relationship and had concluded it was actually a way to manipulate consumption and control price. While automobile manufacturers are required to track and improve their fleet's miles per gallon (MPG) ratings, each year the producers of gasoline have the ability to shave off as much as a tenth of a mile per gallon at their whim by simply tweaking the octane level of the gasoline stock or by adding or depleting the additives used in their product.

Here's a case in point: I remember the advertisements from Shell and Chevron citing their "nitrogen-enriched" gasoline as a way to clean the engine, help it last longer, and an implied but unstated MPG improvement. What's interesting about nitrogen, however, is it is nonflammable and does not support combustion. So, does it really have a reason, then, to be included in the fuel for an internal combustion engine? Nitrogen makes up just over 78% of the breathable air in the atmosphere. Why add more to gasoline?

Another additive I researched has actually been around for over 100 years, namely ethanol. The first Model T was designed to run on either ethanol or gasoline. This was intentional as gasoline was not available everywhere so farmers could produce their own fuel as just another batch of moonshine. The energy content of ethanol, however, is about one-third less than gasoline, meaning at a 10% mix ratio, the MPG would be about 3% less than pure gasoline. As a renewable biofuel, ethanol is more economical than crude oil, but only up to a certain point. When you factor in the energy content of ethanol, however, the price of crude can be much higher than it is today to ward off the exclusive use of ethanol as a full substitute.

My task was to categorize additives in a way that would allow a non-petrochemical professional to immediately know what additive to use and when, without actually needing to understand the underlying chemistry, only its economic impact. This led me to formulate three categories: Accretive, Depletive or Placebo. I came up with these category names to describe their impact on gas mileage and/or engine performance. Nitrogen fits into the Placebo category; ethanol fits into the Depletive category. Nitromethane and Nitrous Oxide fit into the Accretive category. Fuel dyes like Solvent Red 24 fit into the Placebo category. Antiknock additives are also mostly placebos since they provide a nice physical and psychological benefit by keeping the engine from knocking or continuing to run after being turned off.

The less glamorous side of my job, and dare I say the boring part, was to be the subject matter expert on the Environmental Protection Agency's List of Registered Gasoline Additives. This list contains 5,105 additives from 1,030 different companies. The additives may be used in gasoline or diesel fuel, and in some cases both. Knowing the additive's cost, the amount of accretive or depletive impact each would have and being able to quickly identify the manufacturer would give us the ability to manage our margin performance in near real time. This made me the most unlikely profit center within downstream by simply incorporating or excluding an additive.

Now here's where it got interesting. I seemed to mostly be called upon at the end of each fiscal quarter about what additives to put into the finished products and then at the start of each fiscal quarter about what additives to remove from the finished products. This cycle worked like a ratchet on the price and by extension on the profit generated by the company. Strong period endings, or soft period landings, were able to be engineered and I was called upon frequently to enable that outcome. I didn't really think that much about the implications of what I was doing because at the end of the day I was just managing ingredients. That was, of course, until the Securities & Exchange Commission, or SEC, wanted to talk with me.

I was approached during lunch at one of my favorite spots, Pappas Bar-B-Q on Westheimer Rd., about fifteen minutes from my office. Obviously, my eating habits were better known than I realized. The two men and one lady sat down at the table across from me and struck up a conversation by asking, "So what's good here?" I answered honestly and said, "Everything! But my go-to choice is the Mixed Platter." Not thinking any more of it, I ordered, they ordered, the waitress brought food to each of our tables and we all started to eat. I was about halfway through my meal when they thanked me for the food suggestion and said it was amazing. They then proceeded to ask me where I worked and what I did. I told them I worked at an oil company in downstream operations, fully expecting them to have no clue about what that was. Boy, was I wrong as they started to ask me questions about additives.

The questions, though, weren't about chemical compositions or individual ingredients; they wanted to know when the decisions to add or remove something from the mix were made. Without thinking, I said, "At the end of the quarter." The words no sooner left my mouth when the two men pulled out their SEC identification badges and moved from their table to mine. I was taken aback and recoiled slightly, not knowing what to expect next. They then proceeded to tell me the questions I was about to be asked were part of an ongoing investigation of general business practices within oil companies and not specific to my company. I also was told that I was under no obligation to respond. They wanted to know who the decision makers were regarding additives and when the preliminary indications and final decisions regarding their use took place. And while they didn't ask for the name or names of the actual people that gave me the instructions, they wanted to know levels, titles and functional organizations.

I was nervous to respond, but more nervous not to. The questions asked were very generic, non-threatening and without pressure. The SEC agents honestly seemed more interested in process than people. It was through their questions that I came to realize what I already knew. Finance, and not Product Management or Engineering, pulled the strings on our mixtures, and did so in a way to primarily support our financial reporting to the street. I noticed that time had started to get away from us and mentioned it was time for me to get back to work. There were no objections to us ending and we parted amicably. As we walked out of the restaurant, the agents asked I not mention our meeting, or what we discussed, with anyone back at the office. I agreed. When I did walk back into the office, no one even noticed that I was back about thirty minutes later than usual from lunch. I sat down at my desk and settled back into my afternoon work routine.

About a month later, it was quarter close, and right on cue I get the phone call about additives, except this time I wasn't told what to do on the call. I was asked to come up to the boardroom. As I headed to the elevator, a flood of thoughts ran through my mind, but nothing could have prepared me for what was about to happen next.

When I walked into the boardroom, the company's CFO was there along with the General Counsel, both of whom I had never met before, along with the two SEC agents I had talked to that day at lunch. They were all talking to each other as I entered. After welcoming me and asking me to sit down, the General Counsel asked if I recognized the two agents and if I recalled talking to them. I answered affirmatively. He then proceeded to ask me what we talked about and what, if any, details were shared regarding the additives process. I explained we didn't talk about mixtures, only about the timing of their introduction. With that, he turned to the agents to corroborate what I just said, and they nodded their agreement.

The CFO then stood up; she thanked me for coming up and for answering the questions. She then turned to the two agents and proceeded to introduce them as members of the company's Corporate Security organization and explained they routinely track and verify the actions of critical personnel. She said that my lunchtime routines were too predictable and that I need to work more on my tradecraft. Not being sure exactly what she meant, but also not wanting to appear uncooperative, I said I would, and then excused myself from the boardroom.

On the way back to my desk, I did a quick internet search on my phone regarding the word, tradecraft, and saw it meant techniques associated with espionage and intelligence. Obviously, I was supposed to be more discreet, more aware of my surroundings, suspicious of new people approaching me, and not visiting the same places with recurring frequency. I also realized that I was considered critical personnel.

After about an hour, my phone rang and this time it was the additive call. This time, the task was to increase top line revenue which meant the use of a depletive item so that octane and mileage would drop, and more gasoline would be sold. I proceeded to issue the online instructions to our global refinery network to blend in more ethanol, up to 9% by volume from the current 2% level. As long we didn't go beyond 10%, we didn't have to report it to our distribution or retail network, or any of the local regulators. I later heard this had exactly the desired effect on our top line results for the quarter and, as it turned out, also had a very positive effect on my quarterly performance bonus.

About two months later, while exploring a new food court and shopping area that just opened by the office, I noticed a couple of people following me from store to store and between the food stalls. After making my food choice and sitting down, these two people chose a table next to mine and just like last time struck up a conversation about food that then turned into a conversation about work. Their questions were a bit more direct and I could tell they were intent on finding out who I worked for and the role I played. Rather than continuing to go along with their probing, I pulled my phone out, placed a call to Corporate Security, turned on the speakerphone function, and proceeded to inform them of what was going on. That simple action was enough to get the two people to quickly pack up and leave, but not without me snapping a picture of them with my phone.

I guess I'll never know who they were, or what they intended to do with the information they were trying to extract from me, but I'm glad my first encounter of this type was with our own Corporate Security staff, because if it hadn't I don't know how this second situation would have turned out.

Special Pricing

special: adjective - better, greater, or otherwise different from what is usual

I work in an office about 500 feet down the hall from the Chief Pricing Officer. Most days, no one comes in and I only go in and out to use the restroom or to grab lunch. Activity spikes when there's a natural disaster and it peaks when there's a man-made disaster. Why? Because it means I get to invoke "special pricing."

Now mind you, the only thing special about the pricing is that I get to increase the price of crude and subsequently increase the price of gas at the pump. To people impacted by my actions, I'm viewed as a pariah, but internally I'm viewed as a profit center. Imagine that: being able to generate more profits because something bad has happened. The cost of extracting the raw material and converting it into the sellable commodity is effectively unchanged but the availability of the finished product and its demand profile has changed, which means we can charge more.

The trick to doing this, if you can call it a trick, is to make the increase seem reasonable without looking predatory. We rely upon many different metrics to test where that crossover point occurs. The easiest test is to see what the previous high price point was. If we're at or near that high price point already then you rely upon what the last disaster increase amount was in both absolute and percentage terms and base the new increase on those.

Additionally, many years ago we developed a disaster rating scale that equates the size, scope and duration of various types of disaster, along with their aftermath, to determine an increase amount. For example, wildfires and tornadoes don't even make the list; floods due to excessive rain are rated less than floods due to breaches in dams; typhoons and hurricanes are rated fairly high, but it depends upon where they occur. If they only impact third-world or low population locations, then they only have a local pricing impact; but if they encroach upon production locations, crude or finished product transportation routes, or large population centers and areas of high product usage, we can increase our prices more. The highest rating goes to man-made disasters with outbreaks of civil unrest, military actions and wars being the highest rating with the largest impact to pricing. As with any rating system, however, there is a level of subjectivity that can be applied, and special circumstances may increase or decrease an event's corresponding impact to pricing. That subjectivity is "above my pay grade" as they say, but it does get applied.

Recurring events, whether they are annual, every two years or every four years, also have an impact on pricing. Things like holidays (Memorial Day, 4th of July, Labor Day, Thanksgiving and Christmas), the Olympics, and presidential elections are all opportunities to increase pricing as well. The basis for increases in each of these cases falls into one or more of the following buckets: increased demand, decreased price sensitivity due to an underlying need, or uncertainty.

On this particular day in the middle of March, I happened to be the only one in the office when the disaster alarm went off. The alarm itself was akin to one of those stroboscopic fire alarms except without the annoying horn. The light flashed above each office door, at the end of the hallway, and on my desk. Protocol dictated that in the event of an alarm, the first thing to do was to activate the electronic door locks to the premises so no one could enter from the outside. That meant I was about to be locked in by myself. The next step was to isolate all telephone lines and to reconfigure the internal data network to block all unsecured and unsolicited incoming traffic. Both of these things had to take place before even finding out what the disaster was.

Once I had completed the disaster protocol, I was then free to query our data collection sources about what was happening. These sources run the gamut from public and private news content providers to governmental sources including some with Confidential and Secret security ratings. Only by combining and comparing multiple sources could the true nature and scope of a disaster be assessed. From there, the disaster's rating can be determined.

Today's disaster was an earthquake off the coast of Japan. In and of themselves, the ratings applied to earthquakes have the widest spread due to all of the variables in play but they're primarily based upon magnitude and location. Small to moderate earthquakes (i.e., magnitude 5.4 or less on the Richter scale) in locations that are well prepared or seismically equipped to handle them would get very low ratings, but the same size earthquake in a location that was not well prepared or with existing infrastructure problems would be rated higher. Strong earthquakes (i.e., magnitude 5.5 or greater on the Richter scale) receive high ratings to account for both the observed and unobserved impacts as well as the immediate or short-term effects and the long-term implications. Based upon the reports coming in on this earthquake, the disaster rating I was about to assign would make this the second-highest rating ever applied.

Since my next step would be to release the rating, I now had to tread cautiously because once a disaster rating is released to upstream, midstream and downstream operations, an immediate impact on pricing takes place. Unfortunately, all of the people "above my pay grade" were locked out, literally and figuratively. I would have to make the call and determine the amount of subjectivity to apply to the pricing impact and what, if any, special circumstances to consider.

Reports were also starting to come in that this earthquake had triggered a massive tsunami in the Pacific, heading for the Japanese mainland, which at some point would reach other coastal communities much farther away. So, I made the decision to release the second-highest disaster rating ever declared, but did so with specific instructions to either maintain or slightly reduce the pricing at all "stream" points.

Upon formally transmitting the rating, the building, voice and data network lockdowns were released. Phones started to ring, the electronic door locks released, and people started to stream back into the office congregating around my desk. My peers were all asking me what it was like to be alone during this crisis; the bosses were asking me why I made the decisions I did. To the first question, I answered it was scary to be alone but because of our process reviews and drills, I was comfortable with what to do. On the second question, no one had an issue with me declaring the second-highest disaster rating level but the instructions to either maintain or slightly reduce "stream" pricing caused some consternation. They said I missed a perfectly viable opportunity to justify an increase in prices and they were afraid I had set a new precedent. They pointed to oil prices falling below $100 a barrel in New York for the first time in more than a week.

What we would later learn is that the tsunami started a catastrophic chain of events that would include the shutdown of three nuclear reactors, damage to over 1,000,000 buildings, destruction of multiple roads and rail lines, and cause a dam to collapse. The death toll and number of people displaced would be staggering. And the aftershocks would be great enough in magnitude to be considered strong earthquakes in their own right.

About two months after the earthquake and tsunami, I was asked to meet with the Chief Pricing Officer and expected the worst. The first thing he said when I walked in was, "How are you holding up?" That struck me as somewhat odd, but I responded, "Fine, I guess." He then proceeded to tell me of a situation he had ten years earlier when he had to make a difficult call about something that had never happened before. While his event wasn't an act of nature, the chain of events it triggered were far reaching and, in fact, had just recently reached its conclusion. After he told me that his disaster was the attacks on 9/11, I was able to connect the dots and understand the scope of what he was telling me. In both of our catastrophes, there was no precedent to follow, no previous decision to leverage. We each had to make the best decision we could at the time with the information available. While his disaster rating was lower than mine, he issued a "high increase" order to the pricing at all "stream" points. As a result, oil prices spiked and gasoline prices in the U.S. also shot up, but only for about a week.

As we wrapped up our conversation, he said the actions I took were exactly correct, despite what anyone might be saying to me now, and that would only become more obvious to everyone in time.

At What Price?
The OPEC Perspective

perspective: noun - a particular attitude toward or way of regarding something; a point of view

This wasn't like the other projects I had been assigned since starting work in OPEC's Production and Pricing department, the organization's focal point for crude oil market management, but it was the first one that would be focused upon disrupting the global oil industry. I was asked to calculate the price per barrel of oil that would inflict enough pain on non-member oil producers that they would be forced to either follow suit with their pricing or shut down.

To start this calculation, I would need to more fully understand the OPEC cost and margin structure in order to know how low we could go. This meant accessing some of the most highly protected and secret pieces of data within the organization. Since all of our expense was based upon extracting crude oil from the ground, the costs incurred to create the physical infrastructure were actually considered sunk costs, that is, previously spent and not directly attributable to current production. I would, however, have to factor in the fixed and variable costs associated with facilities upkeep and staffing the various extraction steps. The fixed cost portion of the extraction process was readily identifiable, but the variable costs were a bit tricky to calculate. The extraction process itself was highly automated and its physical staffing did not scale in direct proportion with output. In fact, at a certain level of output, the staffing cost per barrel actually went down.

In the course of doing my research I had found records going back to March 1946 and saw the price per barrel at that point was $16.50. Production costs at that time were about three-quarters of that price or $12.38 per barrel. The extraction process was fairly rudimentary at the time with process automation, environmental protection and personal safety concerns not even being on the drawing board. As the post-WWII demand for oil and gasoline increased, the need for more efficient extraction methodologies also increased. The tasks and costs of building those capabilities fell mostly to the largest consumers of the output, namely the U.S., Japan, and mainland Europe. Two other low-price points have occurred since 1946; $20.74 per barrel in July 1973 and $17.66 per barrel in November 1998. By these two dates, the production costs had dropped substantially to $9.28 and $6.19 per barrel, respectively. Today, at full capacity, our cost was $3.71 per barrel equivalent of Brent Crude, one of the three benchmark standards for crude oil.

With this cost profile I was now in a position to determine the price per barrel that would accomplish the desired objective of inflicting the maximum harm on non-member oil producers. It was $18.82 per barrel. This price still provided member producers with sufficient margin to operate in a "business as usual" mode, satisfying both their business and political stakeholders.

My modeling process also calculated another price at the other end of the spectrum, the projected price per barrel of oil that would force someone to seize control of the Arabian Peninsula. Internally, we called it the IN-Price or invasion price.

Interestingly, while the mathematics to calculate the price were relatively straightforward, the actual invasion price point is dependent upon everything from the prevailing political and military climate to the personal predisposition of the decision makers. The best way to understand this phenomenon is to look at a parallel situation like the one Japan faced in 1940.

In 1940, Japan invaded French Indochina in an effort to control supplies reaching China. The United States halted shipments of airplanes, parts, machine tools, and aviation gasoline, which was perceived by Japan as an unfriendly act. The U.S., however, did not stop oil exports to Japan at that time in part because prevailing sentiment in Washington was that such an action would be an extreme step, given Japanese dependence on U.S. oil, and likely to be considered a provocation by Japan.

The U.S. did cease oil exports to Japan in July 1941, following the Japanese expansion into French Indochina after the fall of France to the Nazis, in part because of new American restrictions on domestic oil consumption. This in turn caused the Japanese to proceed with plans to take the Dutch East Indies, an oil-rich territory.

The attack on Pearl Harbor was intended to neutralize the U.S. Pacific Fleet and protect Japan's advance into Malaya and the Dutch East Indies, for access to natural resources such as oil and rubber. As we all now know, the attack was interpreted very differently in Washington, D.C., and, in turn, used for a very different purpose.

So why is knowing this important? Because the IN-Price by itself is not the only consideration. Access to, and control of, the natural resource takes precedence over the price per barrel of oil. Now, how do you go about modeling that? This would be my next challenge and it would require me to tackle this work assignment in a new and unfamiliar way.

I started by looking at the geography of the Arabian Peninsula, including all points of ingress and egress, to formulate a probabilistic model of access. Next, I set up a matrix model for all of the wellhead points of extraction. My inspiration for the matrix was an imported version of the Battleship game I was gifted many years ago, except I also weighted the cells based on the flow capacity of its associated wellhead. The final dimension of my model was to score the political and military climate of potential aggressors as well as the personal predisposition of their decision makers. By far, this dimension would prove to be the most imprecise.

As I ran the model to start simulating various IN-Price scenarios, I noticed several things. First, the higher flow wellhead sites that were closest to the points of ingress by the most probable aggressor resulted in lower IN-Prices than those sites that would be more difficult to access. Second, the political and military climate of an aggressor could overshadow either the wellhead's proximity or its flow. And third, the more volatile a potential aggressor's decision makers were, the lower the IN-Price would be overall.

When I presented my model and simulations to the department's leadership, the very first question they asked me was why I went beyond the original request. I told them I hadn't intended to do so, but in order to have an accurate mathematical model it needed to calculate the price per barrel from low to high as both points would likely trigger some type of reaction. Everyone was pleased to know the low-end price but they seemed most concerned with, and surprised by, the high-end price. Everyone had always assumed an IN-Price would be associated with the United States. My answer in the moment, however, was that the analysis shows them to not be the risk. When pressed further, I displayed a list of fifteen other countries with a lower IN-Price than the U.S. and then spent the next thirty minutes providing the reasoning. After I was done talking, the room sat there in stunned silence. You see, the top five countries were other OPEC members and the implication was that they would turn on their own organization first.

Political Interference Division

Interference: noun - a hinderance or impediment to accomplishing something

We had finally arrived. The U.S. press had to publish stories about how the president does not control gas prices. My years of mass miscommunication, planting questionable stories and false information, spinning blog discussions, wining and dining lobbyists, reporters and writers, had convinced the American voting public that the president did control gas prices.

And, of course, to ensure voting went our way to re-elect the president, we made sure gas prices came down before, during and immediately after the election by increasing the production of crude oil and causing the price per barrel to drop. What's more amazing about it was that this was done amidst the unrest in Syria and Israel's recent use of missiles to signal their discontent with stray mortars; both events that usually would have increased gas prices. If you don't believe we're manipulating the price of crude and gas by now, you likely never will.

We're all familiar with the concept of interference. Before cable, over-the-air television broadcasts were subject to interference from storms. In the days where AM radio was the only kind of radio in your car, passing through a tunnel or between tall buildings would cause interference. Pass interference is a penalty in football and can be either offensive or defensive. Fan interference can change the outcome of a baseball game. Cell phones are subject to interference when driving through areas with spotty coverage. Electromagnetic interference can be caused by power lines and sunspots. In all of these cases, interference disrupts what happens between transmitter and receiver, the quarterback and tight end, or the fly ball and outfielder.

One thing I remember from my physics classes and the labs we did on wave motion was that transmitted waves bend around obstacles and propagate by bouncing off of non-absorbing surfaces. Wave motion transfers energy without displacing particles in the medium without transferring mass. When the waves are disrupted, interference may ensue. But there's also another use of interference that may surprise you. If one wave is in direct opposition to another wave it can negate the other; two waves moving together can combine to make a single larger wave. While this is an over-simplification, I could use these principles to my Division's advantage.

My first initiative was to stall a House bill currently in committee from getting to the House floor. What made this one unique was that we, and the Administration, were supporting the House bill. The stall attempt, however, was meant to only delay and not kill the bill. Navigating that path would be tricky. The reason for delaying was simply to find a more favorable time for the bill to be voted on. To create interference in this case, we'd need to have the representatives from oil-producing states ask for a review and editing opportunity of the current bill. Additionally, we'd want the various petroleum industry organizations to apply pressure on the bill's sponsors and the bill's content, but only enough to extend the debate and prolong the discussion. To start this process required me to work the phones five mornings in a row and go to the Hill every afternoon. In the evenings, I was either overeating red meat at Sam & Harry's or having too much to eat at RPM Italian. I even had to have a few clandestine meetings in front of the SR-71 plane at the Udvar-Hazy Center near Dulles. My efforts paid off. The interference we inserted into the process bought us the time we needed to ensure that when the bill made it to the House floor, it would easily pass.

Another initiative that did not work, and was actually doomed from the outset, was to interfere with the release of several stories that were about to appear in *The New York Times*, *Washington Post*, the *Chicago Tribune* and *Los Angeles Tribune*. The interference we were hoping to insert was not to block the stories but to exploit them. Our Public Relations and Marketing organization had gotten wind of some problems a particular refiner was having with their largest refinery that would be worthy of a press release. The only thing was that the information was somewhat aging and allowing the refiner to fly under the public's radar, meaning it did not have an impact on gas prices. Despite the fact we were being asked to shore up the loss of supply, we would not be able to increase our prices at the risk of looking like we were money hungry. Had the story broken in the press in a timely fashion, gas prices would have been able to go up under the cover of a supply disruption and we would have made more money.

Now you might be wondering why the word "Political" appears in the name of my organization. I know I did before I joined the group. The reason became evident to me after working in the role for a couple of years. "Political" here did not mean governmental politics, although we did our fair share of interference in that arena. The politics we interfered with were socio-economic. All the way back to my high school days and first sociology class, where we learned about everything from city planning to the education system, the underlying context was interconnectedness and cause/effect relationships. Identifying effects and their root cause would give you control of the outcome, or at least put you in a position to predict them. Control is ideal, prediction is good, too; however, the ability to do either is just slightly above 50%.

Our division was only as good as its last interference operation, so we often were in the position of having to run interference for ourselves. While it wasn't particularly productive since it was all internal, the fact of the matter is that it did help build our brand. On this one occasion, we had to pitch the value of our role to Engineering. I knew this would be a tough audience since their approach to business problems used the scientific method and, by definition, was numerically analytical. Nonetheless, I had to come up with a storyline. For this session, I was going to use an example from their space, namely design reviews and the securing of a build budget, with a touch of sports. I characterized the build budget as a ball the outfielder or receiver is trying to catch and how interference, or the lack thereof, can make it harder or easier. They all understood the "harder" concept by virtue of having something block their ability to get funding but couldn't grasp the "easier" concept. I think the word "interfere" was stuck in their minds, so I asked the group if they ever needed to receive signal data from a piece of hardware that was just too hard to discern. As expected, they all shook their heads in agreement. Next, I asked them how they solved the situation. They said either through filtering out the noise or bolstering the desired signal's strength. I explained that both of their solutions were a form of interference by improving the quality of what they wanted to be received.

I later heard the Engineering group had taken my interference concept to heart and had increased their success rate in securing funding from 60% to 90%. That was an outcome I couldn't have predicted.

The Best Defense is a Strong Offense

defense: noun - the action of defending from, or resisting, attack

offense: noun – an aggressive projection of force to occupy territory, gain an objective or achieve some larger strategic, operational, or tactical goal

The closed-door strategy session in the Roosevelt Room at the White House had just concluded. For the first time, a serious discussion about energy independence had taken place and a new direction had been set. Talk about turning the tables . . . the decisions made were clear: 1) Make the U.S. the world's top producer of oil by 2025; 2) Become a net exporter of oil by 2030; and, 3) Be nearly self-sufficient in energy by 2035.

To do this, we needed to create an official-sounding name, meaning one with its own acronym, tied to an acronym-laden organization and a pervasive vehicle to get the word out. Determining the vehicle to get the word out would be easy. The working press would be our unwitting accomplice for information dissemination. The choice of an acronym-laden organization led us actually to two: The Department of Homeland Security (DHS) and the Department of Energy (DOE). We chose the name Homeland Secure Energy Division (or HSED).

The article citing the meeting's decisions broke in the *Los Angeles Times*. The reaction was better than expected. National press picked up the story quickly but the reaction in the Middle East, Venezuela and China was disbelief, followed by a wave of information countering the claim. Words of vast reserves in the Arabian Peninsula, far larger than originally reported, and plans for wholesale refinery expansions and the ability to provide rapid production exposed resources that we all knew were there, but no one had ever spoken about.

It was the master of all bluffs and it played out in a fashion no one could have predicted. The market reacted quickly, but more importantly, global sentiment shifted dramatically. A once scarce and decreasing resource from a part of the world that people feared was exposed for what it was, a plentiful commodity that was being artificially manipulated by a deceitful and clandestine network of wealth brokers operating in a tribal society with a political system akin to the kingdoms of medieval times.

While political and geographic sovereignty would be respected, economic manipulation of the world's life blood would no longer be tolerated. And while it didn't occur to us when we created our name, the press used it to describe what happened to these countries and their oil production monopolies. They were HoSED!

Off Shore

offshore: adjective - a location outside of one's national boundaries, whether or not that location is land- or water-based

Our platform was about 17 miles offshore doing shallow water drilling. We had been stationed here about two years when the call came in from Oil Field Command Ops. It was time to blow the rig. Not surprising timing considering we had been offline and capped for several weeks. They just couldn't afford another spill in this area after the Deepwater Horizon debacle.

Exploratory and drilling initiatives were important to provide a view towards continued supply and support the prospect of continued consumption. Every once in a while, however, the specter of an interruption to supply was needed to bolster prices or at least keep them from falling.

The cycle for these episodes is about 24-36 months and now it was our turn. I had been on four other rigs in the last 10 years and avoided being where the call came in up to now. Rookie platforms would be the most likely targets and easy to explain away as human error, but the preference was to select either the most automated drilling situations or the ones with the most experienced staff. Reason being, the likelihood of a problem there was lower, so if something happened, an accident could be blamed on a failure in technology or a gap in our complex, yet routine, safety mechanisms, but not human error.

To stage the event, we needed to make sure all assets, human and technological, were out of harm's way. The systematic removal of expensive testing and monitoring equipment had already begun as part of the capping initiative. We were also left with a skeleton crew of ten people counting myself. There was also a specific way to blow the rig, making sure the actual cause would be difficult to figure out and the point of origin couldn't be identified. While I never practiced or documented this process, it was known by all my peer Platform General Managers and was passed verbally from one to the other. It even had a code name, "Purple Rain," like the Prince song, but the significance of "Purple" was the key. You see, purple is the highest, and worst, level of alarm on an offshore oil platform, indicating a catastrophic failure situation.

When the time came for Purple Rain, I assembled my nine-member crew in the Ward Room for a routine meeting about our formal abandonment of the platform in two weeks. We reviewed the staging of personal effects, their positioning and order for helicopter pick-up. As I had previously placed the nine timed explosive devices the night before, I didn't need to be anywhere else than with my men at the time of detonation. I watched the clock in anticipation of the series of large explosions that were about to happen, but they didn't. As I adjourned the meeting and the men went back to their stations, I became very nervous that the devices would go off while everyone was spread out over the platform. Fortunately, that didn't happen either.

So why didn't the devices go off? Was I being set up, or were there technical problems? I was going to have to check them and their settings to determine why they didn't function. When I approached the first location, something didn't look right. It was not as I had left it the night before and there was no device to be found. The second location looked like I had left it but upon closer inspection there was also no device. This was the same state of affairs for each of the remaining locations. Someone had stopped the rig from being blown and my ability to execute upon the order I received was not going to be possible without the devices.

Now what was I supposed to do? I couldn't ask the men because it would expose the plan but at the same time it had to be one of them that disabled and removed the devices. There was no way to inspect their personal bunks as that would draw too much attention, and there were so many places to hide things on the rig that I'd never find the devices even with unlimited time. So, I went back to the personnel office and files to see if there were any clues as to who might have done this. While each man's information looked basically the same, two had some interesting backgrounds and work experience. Art was a former SEAL and another, Vince, had worked at multiple other companies as a Platform General Manager. Vince seemed like the best candidate to start with.

The next day, during my rounds, I started at Vince's station. Everything seemed normal with him when I walked up, from his demeanor to the work he was performing. I asked him if he was ready to be back on land and he said, "Definitely!" Then we started discussing his previous employers, their rigs and how he liked being a Platform General Manager. He said the work was good, but he had a problem with doing everything his bosses had asked him to do. That, in fact, is what he said led to his termination. Since he had a pair of headphones around this neck, I used that to start a conversation about music. It was at this point that I asked him if he liked the song "Purple Rain," to which he responded, "I like all Prince music." The only indication he knew what I was talking about was his quick wink at me. Unfortunately, that wasn't enough to implicate him in the removal of the bombs as he may have only been acknowledging the fact he knew what Purple Rain meant from his time as a Platform General Manager.

My next stop was Art's station. He had a combination of inside and outside duties and I happened to find him inside. As I approached him from behind, I was struck by how all of Art's movements were so precise, likely the result of his military training. When he finally heard my footsteps, he turned quickly and snapped to attention with his usual, "What can I do for you, sir?" I answered honestly and said, "Nothing," and that I was just checking in. He didn't seem to buy it, however, and immediately broke eye contact with me. That also wasn't enough to implicate him either, but it provided me with an entry point to ask about the work he was doing and his capping steps. The answers all came back in line with his assigned duties. He even went so far as to articulate the timing and sequence of various steps over the last two days right up to the time of departure. As we wrapped up and I headed to the next station, I realized I was no farther along in finding out what happened last night.

I continued making my rounds with the other seven team members and found no anomalies in what they were doing or in their reaction to my visit or our conversation. I also noticed nothing out of place across the rig until I got to the spiral staircase leading down to the water line and boat mooring. On the very last step, I could see what looked to be a rope tied off and holding something. The other end of the rope led underwater. Not knowing what it could be holding, I reached down and started pulling. At the end were three large nylon fishnet bags. As they moved closer to the surface, I immediately recognized their contents; they each held three disarmed bombs. I let go of the rope and, as the bombs sank back down into the water, wondered who had put them here. And why did they stop Purple Rain?

Since the staircase was on my regular route, I knew I wasn't going to have to explain what I was doing to anyone. And no one was around when I pulled up and released the nets, but I had forgotten about the motion-activated camera on the staircase that fed a monitor at Vince's station. By the time I got back to the Ward Room, Vince was waiting for me. Before I made it through the door, he asked me about the rope and the nets. It was apparent he didn't know what they were, so I told him. While he wasn't surprised about the bombs themselves, he was as shocked as I was about them ending up in the water. Neither one of us could figure that out especially since we both knew the Purple Rain protocol.

The next day, Vince suggested I rotate everyone's station, so I gave out new assignments as people arrived for assembly. The thought process was that, by injecting this change into the mix, the guilty party might be put just enough off-balance to expose themselves. During my rounds, I tried to detect team members acting differently, but frankly, I didn't see or notice anything or anyone out of sorts, so it was time to change tactics. That evening, I went back to the spiral staircase and retrieved one of the nylon fishnets and the three bombs it contained. I placed the three bombs in their original spots but did not re-arm them. Not having the six others to detonate at the same time would only damage the rig and not destroy it.

In the morning, following assembly and rounds, I went to inspect the three locations I had placed the bombs. Just like the last time, the sites all looked unchanged, but the bombs were gone. Obviously, someone was watching my every action and reversing the steps I had been instructed to take. To satisfy my curiosity, I went back to the spiral staircase just to see if the bombs were back in another nylon net. They were. That told me it was time to call Command Ops and let them know what was happening. Given the nature of this communication, I would need to use the secure satellite phone.

Upon entering the communications center, I could tell something was amiss. Not in the obvious "things thrown everywhere and drawers open" kind of way; in fact, it was quite the opposite. The center looked more pristine than I ever remember seeing it. Clipboard logs were all properly ordered and hung on their wall hooks, receivers were in their standby modes and the green light on the emergency beacon was glowing, indicating it was armed and ready. Unfortunately, the only things missing were the Drake desktop and Shure handheld microphones normally attached to each of the radio units. Without those, we could only receive and not transmit. I walked over to the file cabinet where the sat phones are kept, dialed in the combination and slid open the top drawer. Fortunately, the three Inmarsat phones were still there.

I took one of the phones from the drawer and walked outside to the helipad. The phone immediately powered up, showed Searching Satellite, and then displayed Ready for Service. I dialed the number for Oil Field Command Ops. It was obvious the inbound caller identification was working because they answered the phone by acknowledging our rig name, "Good afternoon, Vermilion. Where have you been?" I asked to speak with the Command Duty Manager, was placed on hold for about a minute, and then was put on the line with what sounded like a conference room full of people. Before I could say a word, someone in the room said, "What happened to the rain?"

I said, "That's why I was calling. Someone keeps moving the rain clouds." The conference room fell quiet. I explained that I knew where the "clouds" had been moved to but didn't know who was moving them.

It was at that point a familiar but unexpected voice came on the phone and said a helicopter would be dispatched to the rig in the morning in order to finalize the rig's closeout. It was intended to extract my nine team members by midday, leaving me the only one on the rig. The unspoken part of the plan, with me remaining behind, was obviously to execute Purple Rain. They asked me if I understood the plan and I answered affirmatively.

That evening, I briefed the men on the plan for the morning and they all said they'd be ready. I told them I'd be staying behind to meet a Coast Guard cutter in the late afternoon carrying one of their inspectors and that I'd be leaving with them. They all understood the sequence of events and didn't ask any questions.

The next day worked like clockwork except, of course, there was no Coast Guard cutter. I retrieved the bombs, placed them in their designated spots, armed them with the predesignated coordinated sequence, and then prepared myself for the explosions. Just before the designated time, I put on my "Gumby suit" and waited for the explosions. When they finally exploded, I quickly found myself afloat in the ocean. There'd be no need for me to notify anyone of the explosion as it would be visible for about 100 miles around. As I waited for rescue, the only thing I could think about was who had been watching me and who moved the bombs. Although it would take some time, I eventually came to the realization that I'd likely never know.

California Dreaming

dreaming: verb - *experiencing a succession of images, thoughts, or emotions passing through the mind during sleep*

California's special type of gasoline is the least polluting gasoline in the U.S. It is also more expensive to produce and more difficult for refineries to make. California also switches to a more expensive gasoline earlier in the summer than other states and reverts to the cheaper winter blend after most other states have already done so. How did this happen? Why did this happen? The how is easy to explain. The why, not so much.

California is a juggernaut. As an independent country, it would have the 7th largest economy in the world. As a consumer of gasoline and petroleum-related products, it would be the 4th largest. As a location for personal automobile usage, it would be the 3rd largest. As a location most concerned about the climate, ecology and pollution, it would be 1st. The confluence of these stats in a liberal and predominantly Democratic state provides a foundation for making choices and doing things that couldn't be done elsewhere. Or could they?

I was deployed to California to start influencing legislators, or better said, to spread fear, uncertainty and doubt (or FUD) regarding the negative health effects of California's special type of gasoline. While the gasoline might be the least polluting type in the U.S., the pollution it does create is three times more harmful than its non-California counterparts, or at least that's what I was supposed to be spreading around. My mission was to leverage Proposition 65, a 1986 proposition that requires businesses to provide warnings about significant exposures to chemicals that cause cancer, birth defects or other reproductive harm. The stickers can be found everywhere and they're so prevalent that there's basically nowhere you can go without seeing one except, that is, on the tail pipe or bumper of a gas-burning automobile. As of 2017, there were 14.6 million cars registered in California, or 14.6 million things missing a Proposition 65 sticker, and since car exhaust includes toxins like carbon monoxide, sulfur dioxide, nitrogen oxides, formaldehyde and benzene, that's surprising.

My approach to spread FUD follows the same steps as have been used throughout history except this time I also have the benefit of social media to act as a magnification factor. The first step is to identify experts willing to make public statements voicing their concern. The quantity of experts available to do this is directly proportional to the amount of money I'd be willing to pay. The second step is to get airtime on the radio or television as well as mention in print media. To accomplish this, I must work the news cycle and recognize where the holes occur that this content could plug. The third step, which is the most difficult, is to get a committee or sub-committee hearing by a local or state legislature. This typically only happens after the first two steps take place unless there's a call to action by the public or as a response to a catastrophic event.

I spent $15,000 on each of my four experts. One expert was a university professor teaching chemistry courses at a local college. She'd had multiple occasions to speak at community events regarding the chemicals covered by Proposition 65 and could easily weave in details about their sources. Another expert was a PhD Chemist from the EPA's National Exposure Research Laboratory in Las Vegas who recently found out he was being forced into retirement by the Agency closing their office. With this one, I had both professional knowledge and personal upset to work with. He frequently was asked to testify in court cases involving personal injuries and damages from petrochemical producers. He could seed his public record testimony with the nuance and innuendo I needed. The third expert was with the California Office of Environmental Health Hazard Assessment (OEHHA), and while they weren't supposed to do work and accept payments like I was offering, their impact would be naturally embedded in their day-to-day work without raising suspicion. The last expert self-identified themselves through their involvement in any and all local protests that had an environmental slant. This person was a "two-fer" in that they also usually ended up getting their protest events covered on television. All four of these experts would need about six months to start making an impact, so at this point I left them alone to do their thing while monitoring their progress from afar.

To start the media coverage, I contacted the CBS2/KCAL9 Investigates Tipline from 15 separate burner phones over a period of 45 days casting doubt on how well the Proposition 65 requirements were being upheld at various locations across the state. I also pointed them to multiple emissions inspection stations with less-than-stellar reputations for accurately calibrating their testing equipment. This also was a "two-fer" in that it linked the targeted chemicals to the pollution caused by automobiles. Tipline investigations can take three to six months to come together so I had to let this one run its own course as well. I would, however, be on the lookout for evidence of random visits to the inspection stations.

In order to be ready for the third step, I started the process of identifying the various local governmental committees, chairs and members in the larger cities across the state. With people identified by name, I'd also need to create separate profiles on each of them to understand their political, business and personal affiliations, and in the case of elected officials, their sources of campaign funding. This process usually takes about 2-3 days per person, so I had my work cut out for me for the next three months.

With all the wheels in motion, a lesser person might have laid back a bit, but not me. I set recurring appointments with my experts and reached out to my producer friends at KCAL9 to get a bead on their investigative story content. The experts' progress was on track, but the investigative story seemed to be stalled somewhere, so that's where I was going to redouble my efforts.

The multiple phone call approach hadn't seemed to work by itself, which meant I needed to provide supporting evidence from alternative sources to support the claims in the calls. I pulled Yelp reviews of emissions stations to point to those locations that provided erroneous results passing cars that would have otherwise failed had the testing equipment been appropriately calibrated. There was also a state-by-state evaluation of their respective emissions testing stations versus their state's cumulative results on improving air quality. More states than not had results moving in opposite directions which was indicative of a more widespread issue than even I initially thought or needed for my FUD campaign. Packaging this content up in a consumable, yet anonymous way, for the Investigates team was going to be the hard part. Rather than sending it over in a plain envelope without a return address, I thought it better to have it hand delivered by a source they trusted.

Over the next two weeks, I spent my time pouring through all of KCAL9's Investigates online videos in an attempt to get to know who the reporters were and to discern if there were any recurring themes or common styles in the stories. What I found was a reliance upon city and state policy makers in both the interviews and formal data. They would be ideal to be my trusted sources. I just had to get the info into their hands. Fortunately, they were more approachable and even receptive to hearing from people like me and my experts, so that process was started.

After a normal amount of soak time, I again reached out to my producer friends to see if an investigative story had been put in motion. It hadn't. Since they knew what I was up to, they were very surprised something hadn't taken hold, but no one was more surprised than me given this kind of approach had worked before. One of them said something to me in passing, however, that stuck in my head: "It's as if someone or something is keeping the Investigates team from starting their process."

Not knowing what that meant, or how to even get underneath it, really bothered me. This "external" force could be coming from a multitude of places. Given what my FUD campaign was supposed to do, interference could be coming from oil companies, automobile manufacturers, regulatory agencies or even consumer interest groups, but there was one entity I would have never guessed.

California has the highest gas prices in the country, even higher than Hawaii. The California price includes 57.8 cents per gallon of state tax and fees, plus another 18.4 cents of Federal taxes. Out of all the players in the mix, the Tax Authority had the most to lose and the least control over the raw material, refined goods, additives, byproducts or usages. Anything that could disrupt that revenue stream or shine more light on the fact that 76.2 cents per gallon were taxes was frowned upon. Since my FUD campaign was going to bring unwanted attention to this cash cow, it had to be stopped. In the mind of the Tax Authority, their worst-case scenario would be the loss of their special gasoline and its higher price, for a lower-priced version and less tax revenue. The neutral case was maintaining the status quo. Their best-case scenario would be third-party confirmation that special gasoline was a necessity.

It was only after my FUD campaign failed and I was reassigned to a new project that I learned about what had happened. You see, the Tax Authority threatened KCAL9 with an audit and additional tax levies unless they had the ability to prescreen and censor editorial content. The Investigates report was one of its censored targets.

Brazil and Ethanol

ethanol: noun - a colorless volatile flammable liquid which is produced by the natural fermentation of sugars

Creating new industries, aligning political parties, focusing on country-wide economic stability, coordinating nationwide distribution networks, legislating the automobile manufacturing industry, building user acceptance. These items are not automatically thought of when you think of Brazil, yet this was the task I managed to pull off over a 40-year period. It is still hard for me to believe, and to date, others have not been able to achieve it. You see, the country decided to develop an ethanol industry and make it a mandatory fuel for their internal combustion engines.

So how did I go about accomplishing this feat?

I enlisted a group of experts to start visualizing the end state: cars that run in-part or totally on ethanol. (We'll leave the automotive design and manufacturing issues discussion for another time.) I also knew, in Brazil, you have to be very familiar with the political parties (there are more than twenty), the legislative and regulatory processes, and be an expert in working the "jeitinho" (pronounced jay-teen-yo), Brazilian Portuguese slang for the way around or short cut. From there, I'd have to make sure ethanol is available at every gas station or, in other words, that ethanol is available at the gas pump. To get to the gas pump, we'd need a network of wholesalers and distributors with the capabilities to move the liquid. Since ethanol is made from sugarcane, a distillation facility is required and, if it is being blended with gasoline, a refinery would be involved. Since sugarcane is grown by farmers, we'd also need a network of farmers of all sizes, and from all corners of the country, with the ability to get the raw materials to the distillation site. In other words, to be successful it had to be a vertically integrated operation. Not an easy task in Brazil, or elsewhere for that matter, since each layer wants to be independent and maximize its own profitability.

If there was ever a situation requiring the need to create win-win situations, establish co-dependencies between adjacent parties in a vertically integrated channel, and leverage symbiotic relationships, this would be it. In fact, it reminded me of a real-world scenario from baseball where, in order to effectuate a player trade to get a specific position covered, four teams were required to do back-to-back trades with each other in order to have the last team trading away the right position player satisfy the first team's need.

In the case of ethanol, several of the entities in this channel would never connect naturally, like a farmer and a gas station operator. This meant I had to create the right combinations of back-to-back "trades." Working from left to right, my ethanol channel would look something like this:

Farmer>Broker>Distiller>Refiner>Distributor>Station Operator

Another way to think about this channel would be to think of it as a value chain where each step between farmer and station operator takes an input and makes it somehow more valuable either through aggregation, manufacturing or distribution. In this value chain, as with a real chain, the overall connection is only as good as the weakest link. As I was setting the industry up, the weakest links were the Distributor and the Station Operator, not because of their inherent capabilities but because of the need to accommodate a new liquid and then scale. Over time, the weakest link moved back to the Refiner who had to establish a way to blend ethanol with gasoline at various ratios depending upon prevailing legislation and the evolution of automobile engines. Eventually it moved all the way back to the Farmer's ability to produce sugarcane and the dependency upon weather and rain which were outside of anyone's control.

One acre of farmland can produce 27-31 tons of sugarcane. That acre of sugarcane yields about 800 gallons of ethanol making it twice as efficient as corn, but it uses 10% more water than corn. With one ton of sugarcane needing about 60-70 tons of water that means an acre of sugarcane consumes 1,755 to 2,015 tons of water. While a good portion of that water will come from natural and controllable ground-based sources, there's always the need for rain. Selecting locations within the sugarcane growing latitudes of 35 degrees north and 35 degrees south and with the proper availability of water in Brazil wasn't going to be all that difficult, but selecting a location with ready ingress and egress was. This is when I knew the "jeitinho" would come into play.

The best location I found literally had no roads going to it, nor did it have any plans to ever have roads, but the one thing it did have that other more accessible locations did not was a local government that knew their way around all of the legislative and environmental obstacles that would undoubtedly come up at the time of development. In fact, their ability to work the "jeitinho" would enable this location to come online faster than any of those with roads already in place. This could not have been more evident than after the location was selected, as all the previously unknown rules and agencies associated with the location surfaced.

City planning in Brazil came to the fore in the late 1950s with the creation of a master planned, new capital city, Brasilia, in the center-western region of the country. This location, on a plateau, had very few inhabitants and little to no infrastructure when selected. It represented a blank slate upon which to create a city. A large artificial lake, Paranoá, was created to increase the amount of water available and to maintain the region's humidity. Our selected location would not need an artificial lake, but it would need the same careful planning for roadways that Brasilia had in order to support the large quantity of agricultural terminals the sugarcane would require. I knew funding to build out this part of the infrastructure would require both governmental and private investment along with extra monies for the various "despachantes" or dispatchers to expedite the whole process. Care would also need to be taken to make sure the "right," meaning politician-owned, companies were used. Fortunately, I knew which ones.

With that part of the value chain coming together, I could focus on the other end of the chain, namely the Distributors and Station Operators. I wouldn't need to worry about Distillers or Refiners as they were already in place and always looking for ways to maximize the use of their facilities, plus sugarcane had been used for making liquor in Brazil for a very long time, an alcoholic beverage called "cachaça." The Distributors were going to require either a new tanker fleet or a new way to partition their existing tanker trucks to carry the ethanol fuel. With the appropriate financial incentives, and the right amount of cajoling by me to stimulate a little competition between the three largest distribution companies, I was able to convince them to start making preparations to transport the new product. The Station Operators were not going to be that easy.

There were three challenges at the gas station end of the value chain: First was the establishment and configuration of storage tanks to hold the new product and pumps to dispense ethanol. Second was market coverage and making sure ethanol was available at all, or at least at most, stations. Third, and most importantly, was the enlistment of the stations' owner-operators. The oil company-owned stations would fall into line somewhat automatically by virtue of their connection to the refineries, but the franchised stations would require special attention. I had previously determined that the last link of the value chain, the Station Operator, had the thinnest margin and, therefore, the least interest in participating. In order to gain their support, I would create a consortium of independent station owner-operators that would work together to price fix a liter of ethanol and build in end-point profit.

I wouldn't have known about this process if it hadn't been for a previous experience in Brazil years earlier when I was part of a U.S.-based corporation's joint venture with a Brazilian electronics firm. I had joined a colleague for what I thought was going to be a casual dinner that surprisingly included all our competitors who were responding to a formal bid from the country's primary telecommunications operator. The reason for coming together was to discuss our bid responses, the pricing we were going to use, and the areas we would each bid upon. When that conversation surfaced, I instructed my colleague that, as part of a U.S. corporation, we couldn't be party to the conversation and had to leave. This time, however, as an independent contractor with no ties to the U.S., my ability to choreograph the consortium was unfettered.

With all parts of the value chain now lined up, the process was ready to be put into motion, but since the growth of sugarcane at volume would take about 12 months, I used the time to practice the hand-offs between the players in the value chain and to scale the operation. During that time, I'd occasionally hear about a link questioning their role and value in the overall transaction and would immediately descend upon them to provide reassurance. Every once in a while, I'd forget my cash-filled briefcase at their office, purchase a new set of football (soccer) uniforms for a local team, or provide a sponsorship for a football tournament or Samba school. In other words, it was Brazilian business as usual.

I reflect back now on what it took to set up this value chain and the amount of time and energy spent to navigate this channel with a product that, at its core, was both economically disruptive and environmentally responsible. I often wonder how I did it. Like most of the challenges faced throughout my career, it required using all of the learning and experiences picked up along the way, the building blocks of knowledge, so to speak, that seem insignificant when they happen, but when stacked together in unique ways enable you to reach new heights of effectiveness that you could never imagine.

Paying at the Pump
(and other places)

*pump: noun - a mechanical device using suction
or pressure to raise or move liquids*

What if the price you paid per gallon was determined by
the distance you drove each month? Or by the amount you
could afford to pay? Or if it was based upon your annual
income? And where does that Gas Guzzler tax end up
anyway?

The Office of Consumer Pricing in the Department of
Commerce ponders these questions, but the group is also
matrix managed by the respective agency of the item(s)
being priced. In the case of gasoline, it is the Department
of Energy, but not the Fossil Energy division. My matrix
manager was in the Intelligence Office.

Gasoline had been declared a strategic resource
in 1975 in a little-known section of the Energy Policy
& Conservation Act (EPCA) making it subject to rules
governing the Strategic Petroleum Reserve (SPR). While
the SPR is publicly advertised to hold crude oil in large
artificial underground caverns made from salt domes near

major centers of petrochemical refining and processing, the gasoline equivalent consists of a nationwide network of above ground holding tanks that are off-book facilities embedded among existing oil, gasoline and natural gas storage tank facilities. The purpose of holding gasoline is to address short-term refinery disruptions that would render the crude oil reserve somewhat worthless.

By managing the price at the pump, one would be able to make sure the investment made in stockpiled gasoline doesn't lose value and only appreciates. Of course, the government received preferential purchase pricing reminiscent of those days in the 1960s when leaded gasoline was $0.27^9/gallon. The Gas Guzzler tax is fully directed at making this purchase but so, too, is the current price at the pump. With each gallon purchased at the pump, the price paid per gallon includes the purchase of one-tenth of a gallon for the reserve. Most people either don't know or realize this, but why would they? As long as the pumps keep pumping and the price stays in the "reasonable" range, people are good to go.

Most days, my job was fairly mundane. People would bring me news reports and market data regarding gasoline consumption, and I'd issue a forward-looking view of the gasoline prices to be used across the country in future weeks. This one day, however, one of the Department's economists paid me a visit that would forever change my thinking on how to set gasoline prices. They suggested a pricing algorithm that would change the price at the pump depending upon an individual's driving characteristics and their ability to pay.

The new algorithm would require a complete remake of the gas pump itself as it would require the computing power, network connectivity and the intelligence to change per gallon pricing based upon the individual making the purchase. The advertised reason was to reward specific behaviors that would ultimately moderate consumption, support renewable sources and reduce the impact on the environment. The real reason was to make the cost of gasoline and its impact on a person's pocketbook commensurate with what someone could afford or, in other words, to inflict comparable amounts of pain to everyone. It was the pricing equivalent of Robin Hood; take from the rich and give to the poor.

As I dissected the algorithm, the following datapoints and comparative characteristics being used surfaced:

Gas Pump Global Positioning System (GPS) Coordinates
Point of Sale (POS) Debit/Credit Card Identification
    Information
Line 11b, 1040 – Taxable income
Annual Odometer Disclosure Statements
Vehicle Registration Cards
State Vehicle Emission Inspection Reports
Home Zip Code
Work Zip Code

I was surprised by the limited number of data elements being used but very impressed with the way they were being combined. For example, the distance between Home and Work Zip Codes formed the basis for non-discretionary daily, weekly and annual mileage. Non-discretionary annual mileage was subtracted from annual mileages recorded on Odometer Disclosures and Emission Reports to calculate discretionary mileage. Vehicle Registration

Cards gave visibility to individual per gallon gas mileage figures and also allowed for the ranking of car types like is done by car rental agencies: compact, economy, mid-size, full-size, premium, sport, SUV, etc. Superseding all of this, of course, was Taxable Income.

High incomes with low per gallon mileage vehicles and long distances between home and work triggered higher per gallon prices than for individuals with low incomes, low per gallon mileage vehicles and long distances between home and work. The lowest per gallon price came with low incomes and high per gallon mileage vehicles; the distance between home and work had no bearing on the matter. Discretionary mileage, and the miles per gallon of the vehicle being driven, could increase or decrease the per gallon price as well, tempered of course by annual income. I wasn't surprised by any of these results. The real surprise would come later.

About a week after learning about the algorithm, I was asked my opinion on doing a limited market trial with it and whether or not I'd be open to working with gas pump manufacturer Gilbarco Veeder-Root. My curiosity got the better of me and I quickly said, "Yes." Given the nature of the work, we needed a non-disclosure agreement, or NDA, with Gilbarco to cover both the algorithm, use case and the potential design considerations for the gas pump itself. I was designated as Project Lead so in my initial meeting with Gilbarco, I laid out the type of network connectivity and computing platform the gas pump would require but did not share the algorithm or intent of the work effort. My team and I would be the ones to write all of the gas pump's computer code to implement the pricing algorithm, but we'd use existing code for the POS and network interfaces.

It took us about four weeks to write and debug the code on the gas pump's Exorcisor, the test bed of the pump's main computer. To start, the algorithm's decision logic required POS data from an inserted debit or credit card to establish purchaser identity and the gas pump's GPS location. This data string would then be transmitted via the network interface to the Commerce Department's mainframe computer in order to combine the received information with the purchaser's socio-economic and automotive characteristics. The algorithm would then calculate a unique price per gallon and transmit it back to the gas pump. This all had to happen between the time it would take someone to put the card away, pick up the gas nozzle, and select the fuel grade. In other words, it had to operate as fast as a Google search. Individuals paying in cash would default to the average price per gallon based upon the pump's average price over the preceding thirty days. That value would be locally maintained and continuously refreshed. A failure in the upstream or downstream network would also result in the pump's average per gallon price being used.

With the technical solution in place, the project's focus shifted to the change management process and communications needed to ensure a successful implementation. How would people react to this type of pricing? What would, or should, a consumer see happen at the gas pump? And what steps would need to be taken to avoid consumer fraud at the gas pump? These were just a few of the questions we'd had to solve for.

On the change management front, the work effort began by creating a list of stakeholders to be impacted and how it would manifest. The consumer pumping gas will immediately see their per gallon price and react either positively or negatively to how it compares with the last time they pumped gas or the prices posted on station signage. Since the bulk of an individual's underlying data wouldn't change between fill-ups, except for the location of the gas pump, once someone's price per gallon was determined it would remain relatively constant. This meant consumers needed to be well-prepared for the first time they received their price. Additionally, the station operator would need to be prepared for onsite customer inquiries about the gas pump's operation and how to handle inquiries about the price, but they would not be required to explain how the price was determined.

For communications, multiple cascading messages in the form of television commercials, gas station and gas pump signage, direct mail, and pocket-sized brochures available at the pump would all be made available. Their common message was predominantly environmental and tied to reducing overall consumption. To support the message, online calculators were created to allow people to enter their own information and assess the per gallon price impact of various changes to their gasoline consumption behaviors. No mention would be made of the Robin Hood methodology, however.

The most daunting challenge was how to prevent fraud. At its most basic level, we'd have to prevent someone with a lower price per gallon purchasing gas on behalf of someone with a higher price. This would be addressed by activating a feature the automobile manufacturers had been building into cars for some time, the Fuel Tank Vehicle Identification Number (FT-VIN) system. Detected upon inserting the gas pump nozzle into the fuel filler connection on the car, the gas pump would recognize the vehicle and validate it with consumer's POS and registration data. If the information aligned, fuel would be allowed to flow. If not, another debit/credit card would have to be used that matched the registered owner of the car. Of course, someone could pay cash and get the rolling 30-day average price but with FT-VIN that would be recorded and the consumer's per gallon price would adjust the next time a debit or credit card was used. Fleet vehicles and rental cars would have their FT-VINs recognized as such and automatically trigger their pre-negotiated gas prices independent of the use of cash or whatever POS information is rendered at the pump.

The first two live market trials were strategically selected to test both the upper and lower limits of the pricing algorithm. I personally worked on the upper limit location. We selected an area in northern California where the prices and income levels were among the highest, the thought being an individual's increase in price there would be least noticed and better tolerated. My counterpart was assigned to the lower limit location, which was in Mississippi where the gas prices and income levels where among the lowest. Here a reduction in price would be well received and immediately noticed.

As the change management and communications plan was put into effect there was no apparent change in consumer behavior or social media traffic. Gas station volume consumption remained at the same levels. Pocket brochures at the pumps were being picked up and oil company credit cardholders in the targeted zip codes received an insert with their monthly bill notifying them of the pending change.

Once the pricing algorithm was turned on, the northern California pricing only increased by two to three cents per gallon and was lost in the rounding of a price that was already over $4 a gallon. In Mississippi, per gallon pricing went down by eight to ten cents per gallon and, with a mid-$2 a gallon price, was immediately noticeable. The reaction there was palpable and generated a buzz.

Each location was subjected to the algorithm for six months in order to see if consumption or purchase volume changed and I was tasked with the data analysis for both so as to have a common approach applied to each for comparative purposes. On the surface, the pricing algorithm, change management and communications plan all worked as expected. There were no observable peripheral effects in the northern California location, but in Mississippi there was an uptick in discretionary spending commensurate with the monies saved on gasoline. I was surprised, however, not to see any changes in driving behaviors or fuel consumption. Perhaps the price changes weren't significant enough or the data analysis I was performing wasn't looking in the right places. My experience told me it was the latter.

The next day I broke the data into weekday and weekend buckets. This time both locations showed changes in driving behaviors and fuel consumption, but only on the weekends. The price increase location saw a reduction in weekend driving and fuel consumption whereas the price decrease location experienced an increase. Obviously, the routine of weekday driving had masked the variability in weekend driving.

The following week, I was supposed to provide a readout on the findings to the Department of Commerce but had to reschedule. For the pricing impact, I had a good data set and was able to draw conclusions from the results, but without the consumer sentiment survey and station operator focus group results, the readout would have been incomplete. Experience had taught me a situation like this required a 360-degree view.

It was a good thing that I waited. As I read the consumer sentiment survey results, I was taken aback by the large quantity of inflammatory verbatim responses written by both groups. The themes from the upper limit location were mostly about how everything costs more in California because of liberal Democratic rule to failed tax programs and to adjust gasoline prices based upon income and affordability was just another way to take money. The themes from the lower limit location were simultaneously appreciative of getting reduced prices but somewhat indignant to the fact someone thought their income or personal situation warranted it. The station operator focus group transcripts spoke to having to spend more time talking to customers, needing to explain how pricing was being handled, and listening to complaints about the per gallon price itself. So basically, both populations had nothing good to say about being subjected to this pricing approach.

At the rescheduled Commerce Department readout, I presented the pricing results data about both locations separately along with their respective sentiment survey and focus group content rather than grouping pricing results data with pricing results data, sentiment surveys with sentiment surveys, and focus group transcripts with focus group transcripts. This allowed a location's reaction to the algorithm's usage to be evaluated individually rather than making it about comparing a price increase location to a price decrease location.

Now for the surprise I mentioned earlier. The algorithm and approach we were asked to test had been around for years but had never been used commercially because the automation to support it didn't previously exist. It had, however, been used to secretly price large volume governmental transactions of refined petroleum products between countries in an attempt to normalize the impact of energy costs between developed and underdeveloped economies. With an advantage on energy pricing, an underdeveloped country would have the opportunity to improve their situation more rapidly than normal. It also reduced the ability of other governments to exploit them or hold them back. Unfortunately, not everyone wanted that to happen.

As a result of successfully completing the two consumer trials, the same phenomenon was now about to play out across the United States. Locations that had been held back or exploited by others via energy pricing were now going to be given an opportunity to improve their situation. Like the government-to-government transaction, however, not everyone wanted that to happen either.

The Role of Reserves

reserves: noun - a supply of a commodity not needed for immediate use but available if required

I was actively recruited from my high-profile investment banking job in New York City to take a nondescript civil service job with the Department of Energy in Washington, D.C. My new salary and bonus opportunity were twice the amounts I'd had in investment banking and well above the highest published amounts on the General Schedule (GS) pay scale. More impressively, the investment I controlled in my new job is one hundred times larger than what I had under my purview in my previous job. It was the Strategic Petroleum Reserve.

Like a savings account, or the so-called "emergency fund," the SPR was first intended to be a safety net for the country. Left silent was the fact it was set up for purely military purposes. Releases from the SPR are under the authority of the President of the United States. Recent examples of these releases were during Operation Desert Storm and following Hurricane Katrina. The SPR also provides a way to normalize supply in periods of peak demand or constrained production. Over time, it has become an investment that increases and decreases in value in much the same way the price of a share of stock fluctuates. Unlike a share of stock, however, this asset can be tied directly back to its raw material. The analogy of dollar-cost averaging applies in this situation as the SPR was stocked in periods of low, medium and high barrel prices. The actual average barrel-equivalent value of the SPR is a tightly held secret but based upon the market price history of oil since the time of the SPR's creation, it is higher than $25 a barrel but well less than $75 a barrel. Like stock, however, knowing when to sell is more important than knowing when to buy.

Unlike my investment banking job where I could make most of the decisions myself, or at least thought I could, this role required me to build Cabinet-level consensus for every purchase transaction. At first, I didn't recognize or buy into this reality and tried to execute my individual orders only to be blocked at multiple points along the way. Over time, I learned to navigate through the labyrinth of stakeholders involved with the SPR transactions. While I didn't like it, it was my reality.

In the process of cultivating relationships within the Department of Energy, Department of Defense and at the Pentagon, I started to detect two unique points of view regarding my job. The first was aligned to the stated reason for the SPR, namely, to make sure resources were available in the event of a military need or an interruption in the supply of crude oil. This struck me as somewhat ridiculous because, from where I sat, if there was something the Government needed or wanted, we had the power—and in certain cases, the right—to go in and take it. The second, and I'd say stronger, point of view was to manage the economy by exerting direct control over the supply and demand for crude oil.

I never really saw this job, or myself, as being all that powerful despite what was being ascribed to me. Perhaps that was a mistake. My staff provides me with daily briefings on the global supply and demand characteristics of crude oil, its associated spot prices, and the prices of all refined materials. I also receive a daily classified Defense Department report citing potential threats to global oil-producing sources. These two data points are the leading indicators I use to assess where problems could come from and where opportunities could exist.

I'm also visited by representatives and lobbyists from the "Oil Majors" on a monthly basis. Their messages are mostly corporate in nature discussing drilling rights, shipping regulations, tariffs and environmental issues. They see the SPR as their personal safety net to provide downside price protection in the event of over-supply and increased profitability at times of high demand. What they don't like is a release from the SPR, a point they mention to me at every meeting. Because of this, protocols are in place to notify the Oil Majors within 24 hours of making the decision to do a release from the SPR. Of course, these protocols are subordinate to the protocols to actually do a release from the SPR.

Every month I am required to sign off on the SPR Inventory. I receive what is basically an Excel worksheet showing the quantity of crude stated as Sweet barrels and Sour barrels. The worksheet also contains a reckoning of SPR Oil Movement in Millions of Barrels citing Exchange Barrels and Drawdown/Sales Barrels to identify the Net

Movement in or out of the reserve. One of the problems with this, and there are many, is the lack of a mechanical gauge to read volume. It is based upon liquid height levels in the four SPR storage sites and their known dimensions. The SPR has the capacity to hold 727 million barrels of oil. In volume, that is 115 million cubic meters. The latest Excel showed us to be at an 87% fill factor or approximately 635 million barrels. In the absence of any Net Movement from last month, I signed the document, but no one expected what I was about to do next.

That night, I decided to see the SPR for myself. The next day, my trip plans had me arriving in Baton Rouge around 9 a.m. and at the Bayou Choctaw storage site about 40 minutes later. It would take me another two and a half hours by car to get from there to the West Hackberry site, and another hour and a half to go to the Big Hill site. The Bryan Mound location, another two hours away, is where I'd end my day. After leaving the first site, I was surprised to learn none of my predecessors had ever visited them or the other three SPR locations. I was further surprised no one at any of the sites was able to show me how and where the liquid height measurement was made. The only silver lining was the access control and site security did work everywhere.

I flew out of Houston Hobby the next day on the late morning nonstop flight back to Washington Reagan. By the time I got back to the building it was quitting time, but everyone was still at their desks. People were heads-down; no one was talking, and no one looked up when I walked in. When I got to my office door, it was closed and the hallway blinds were shut, but I could hear muffled voices coming from inside. Upon opening the door, the voices stopped, and I found myself face to face with the Secretary of Energy and the Secretary of Defense. Apparently, my little road trip had struck a nerve.

Neither one of them stood up when I walked into my office. They didn't say a word, but then again, they didn't have to. I finally understood what was meant by "if looks could kill." I walked around my desk, put my briefcase down, and could only think of one thing to say: "Gentlemen, what can I do for you?" Not a bad opening line, but the response I got was better: "How was your trip?" I immediately knew they knew what I knew they knew. So I answered, "Fine, but I should have spread the visits out over two days." And that's when the rapid-fire questions started. "What made you want to visit the sites? What did you think of the facilities? How was the staff reception when you arrived? Who did you see? Did anything surprise you? How were the roads and traffic? Did you eat any crawfish? Did you tell anybody about what you saw?"

It was very obvious the last question was the most important one in the whole bunch. So, I said, "Here's my answers in reverse order: No, no, fine, yes, onsite staff, good, very impressive, because I wanted to see what I was being asked to approve." This was a trick I had learned a long time ago to both demonstrate I was listening to the questions but also to show I wasn't intimidated and could answer honestly by answering fast. As much as their rapid-fire questions had attempted to disarm me, my rapid-fire answers had disarmed them. The answer they came back to was the one about needing "to see what I was being asked to approve." Apparently, no one had ever verbalized that before let alone taken it upon themselves to go visit the sites.

That singular step, however, put me into a select group of people, the group that knew the truth about the SPR.

Both Cabinet members stayed with me for about an hour. We talked about the facilities, the strategic and military importance of the SPR, the value and importance of secrecy, and my future career with the government. They both said I could contact them on their private office numbers whenever I needed to, but they stopped just short of saying I could write my own ticket from now on. This fact was strongly implied, however. By the time they left my office, the rest of the floor was empty, and it was dark outside. I sat at my desk for another thirty minutes to let the events of the last two days sink in, but one thing kept bothering me. I knew the crude oil volume purchase transactions were real, so where was all that oil?

The next day, back in the office, people were buzzing about having both the Secretary of Energy and Secretary of Defense in my office. I'm sure everyone wanted to know why, but no one had the nerve to ask. I tried to go about my business as usual, but it was hard not be distracted. Where was all that oil? Fortunately, at the office, I had access to several secure terminals used for budgeting, inventory management and primary research. As such, inventory would be my starting point.

Since I knew the recent crude oil purchase history and had approved those orders, my search began there. The order quantities, points of origin and bills of lading were all as expected. The port registrations and off-loading summaries also aligned with the flow meter and volume measurements per location. In other words, everything looked in order. That was, at least, until I noticed the point-to-point pipeline designations. We were supposed to be using the DOE 40", Shell 20" and Shell 24" pipelines to access the SPR storage sites but saw that the Permian Express pipelines were in play. This meant that the crude was being placed somewhere other than one of the four SPR sites. As I dug in further, the orders that preceded my arrival on the job also referenced pipelines that went to unlikely places. I made mental notes of the orders and pipelines in play and thought this would be perfect fodder for my first phone call to one of my Cabinet member contacts.

Back in my office, I originated an encrypted call to the Secretary of Defense. He answered his phone immediately. After exchanging pleasantries, instead of asking why I was calling, he said he expected my call and knew what was bothering me, namely "where was all that oil?" Before I could say a word, he asked me a question, "Do you think we'd tell the world where we kept the real strategic petroleum reserve?" I said, "No, I guess not." I thanked him for taking my call and we hung up.

Years later, as I think back about my time with Energy, I was very naïve in the ways of national security. The SPR was a textbook example of governmental deception at a grand scale. Knowing this kind of misdirection was possible prepared me well for my work at Langley. I just never thought I'd be the Director of National Intelligence.

ODI

*disinformation: noun - false information which
is intended to mislead, especially propaganda
issued by a government organization to a rival
power or the media*

The Department of Energy's Office of DisInformation, or
ODI, was responsible for making sure what people thought
were the reasons for what was happening in the market for
oil and natural gas looked nothing like the real reasons. In
today's world, they'd call it the Department of Fake News.

Creating disinformation was not as hard as it sounded.
In fact, most of it seems more plausible and logical than
real information. It was certainly more interesting. But the
best part of disinformation is that it spreads about ten times
faster than real information with one-tenth of the effort.
Members of the Working Press can be counted on for the
dissemination step but are not as fast to believe what they
see or hear. That's where the real work of ODI comes in.

Fabricating stories from actual events, about real
people, or with real information, is all about interpretation
and misconnecting the dots. Linear, or cause and effect,

thinking can be easily misdirected by providing large amounts of irrelevant data and supporting information that cannot be easily sorted or eliminated. People who think vertically are selective, analytical and sequential. People who think laterally use an indirect and creative approach with reasoning that is not immediately obvious. ODI was able to influence both.

Conspiracy theories can always be counted on to develop on their own and require the least amount of work. One of the best examples in the recent past took place in December 2014. Russian President Vladimir Putin took to the airwaves and floated the idea that the oil price drop was the result of a U.S.-Saudi plot to hurt his country. "We all see the lowering of the oil price. There's lots of talk about what's causing it," Putin said. "Could it be the agreement between the U.S. and Saudi Arabia to punish Iran and affect the economies of Russia and Venezuela? It could." A story in *The Washington Post* not only picked up on President Putin's remarks but gave legs to the use of conspiracy theories as a way to misdirect people's thinking. The ODI benefitted from both Putin's remarks and the *Post*'s response because both were correct despite being hard to believe on the surface.

I wasn't exactly sure how or why I received the job offer from the ODI's Verification Division but learned long ago not to look a gift horse in the mouth. I had just finished my Master of Fine Arts degree at Washington University in St. Louis. During my time as an English major, I published several works of fiction and even won several writing contests. One of my winning stories, however, obviously struck a nerve and caught the government's attention. It was a story about a land developer in the Coachella Valley of southern California who built resorts, golf courses and timeshare properties using long-term leases on government-controlled Indian and fee land in order to protect mineral rights. What people didn't know was the idea for this story came from a former Provost and his earlier relationship with a university Controller who had changed careers and was now doing land development. The concept of using above ground construction to preclude drilling and geo-seismic research was the basis for my story's plot and a perfect example of misdirection.

What I didn't know about my fictional story was it turned out to be true. The mineral rights being hidden were in a 24-mile-long, 4-mile-wide oil field along the lower southwestern half of the 47-mile-long, 15-mile-wide Coachella Valley. The Bureau of Indian Affairs and the resident Agua Caliente band of Cahuilla Indians were not even aware of this. The developer had never been in the military or intelligence community and was the least likely individual to be doing off-the-books work for the Department of the Interior. Because of my ability to write fictional stories that turned out to be true, my job in the Verification Division was to make sure others writing fictional stories weren't knowingly or unknowingly doing the same thing. If a fiction writer did stumble across the truth, my job was to first determine if they knew the truth or not, and then find out where their idea came from. The role of ODI would then be to voice concern about the content as either a risk to national security or as a complete fabrication. The more ODI raised concerns about a fictional story, the more attention it would get, and the more people would start to believe it to be true. Stories that were true and didn't get ODI's attention were written off as being harmless. This is what made my job in ODI so important. The verification step determined the position ODI would take. Being a writer was thought to help my ability to discern fact from fiction and being able to find cues in the text. I was basically doing a counter-intelligence job, or better said, a counter-counter-intelligence job.

After about two years, they moved me to the Creative Division. Here I was tasked with crafting the believable fictional stories that formed the base of ODI's propaganda. Most of my assignments were fairly simple and short. They were used as fillers by most of the major papers and occasionally would get a passing mention on local broadcast news but never really had a global reach. That was until I was handed the rare earth minerals scarcity story.

The two sides for this story were internal combustion engines and electric cars. On the side of internal combustion engines were the global oil companies and the entire vertically integrated petrochemical industry. On the side of electric cars were the environmentalists, the specialty mining industry and the sites associated with the rare earth minerals that comprise their batteries.

The competing perspectives for this story were the availability of crude oil, the impact of burning fossil fuels and the scarcity of rare earth minerals.

Normally, when I compose a piece of propaganda, there are two distinct vantage points to consider and one is trying to either prove or disprove the other. This time there were at least three different points of view. Automobiles using fossil fuels were bad for the environment. Electric cars with zero emissions were neutral to the environment in and of themselves but still required the burning of fossil fuels to drive the electricity grid required to charge them.

The batteries storing the energy were dependent upon rare earth minerals that were in limited supply and in locations that were politically sensitive. Spinning a story of scarcity or difficult access would drive the price of batteries up making the cost of the electric car higher than its internal combustion counterpart. A story of an abundance of crude oil would drive the price of gasoline down making the transition from internal combustion to electric vehicle more prolonged. The extraction of an abundant resource, namely oil, from the ground, or the exploitation of a scarce resource, namely rare earth minerals, both had a negative environmental impact but at different points in their respective lifecycle.

So, would the position be to support or deny the scarcity of rare earth minerals? By supporting their scarcity, I'm increasing their price and the downstream products that rely upon them. Citing the negative impact they have on the environment would decrease their value and make the use of batteries less attractive. By offering an alternative to internal combustion engines, I'd be driving the price of gasoline down and prolonging the use of conventional automobiles. It was always from this kind of back and forth, or point/counterpoint, that I could frame my point of view for the propaganda. In this particular case, I would focus on the environmental aspects of the two competing technologies and divert attention away from the availability of rare earth minerals, where they came from, or what was going to have to be done to secure them.

Surprisingly, my article was picked up by major newspapers in San Jose, Detroit and Washington, D.C., along with the Society of Automotive Engineers, the Institute of Electrical & Electronics Engineers, *World*

Oil (formerly *The Oil Weekly*) and *Mining Magazine*. Apparently, I had threaded the needle between competing technologies in a way that both sides could use the article to support and promote their positions. In this case, my disinformation initiative diverted attention away from both natural resources whose extraction and use had negative consequences while not making one look more attractive than the other so as to draw undue attention.

I had never really considered the other purposes ODI could have until I was asked to write a historical narrative about the war in Vietnam. For this request to come up 38 years after the war ended was odd enough, but to come on the heels of my article about rare earth minerals turned out to be more than coincidental. As I started to do the research for my article and determine the position to support, I ran across some natural resources statistics that surprised me. Vietnam is tied for 2nd in the world behind China in its reserves of rare earth minerals. Could the stated reason for the U.S. involvement in the Vietnam War, namely, to keep communism from spreading throughout southeast Asia, have a been a disinformation campaign to mask the desire to take over a rare earth mineral-rich location? Did someone have the foresight regarding the future importance of those minerals? And, if so, who? The answer would end up pointing all the way back to the Kennedy administration, but the real escalation in Vietnam occurred during Johnson's presidency. With Johnson being from Texas, the largest oil-producing state in the Lower 48, it started to feel as if my narrative was starting to write itself, but I was concerned. I had stumbled into another situation like my winning story about Coachella Valley, except I didn't know how people would react to this one being told.

TNBT

TNBT: acronym – the next big thing

I've been out of school for six years and working professionally for four years in my chosen career of forensic accounting. The one course I expected the least from and took as an elective from the Engineering Department and their Technology & Human Affairs program, however, has turned out to be the most critical in my day-to-day work. We learned about the identification and valuation of crude oil reserves measured in quads, a unit of energy equivalent to 8,007,000,000 US gallons of gasoline or 25,200,000 tonnes of oil.

Once crude oil has been extracted from underground or refined into gasoline it is easy to measure. For oil still underground or considered reserves, the measurement is more difficult as it is masked by geology. Indirect techniques attempt to size these reserves using the technology of the day. Reserves are classified either as Proven or Unproven. Terminology describing both has been developed but is subject to the uncertainty that production, technology, commercial, regulatory and political conditions create.

My forensic journey started when I questioned an asset entry my company used to secure a large bond being used to fund economic diversification in anticipation of our crude oil reserves running out. I was told that my emirate had only 40 years of reserves left and that we needed to start investing in other industries for when the oil ran out. An adjacent emirate is said to have 80 years of reserves so their need to diversify was a bit farther out. The part I couldn't figure out is why to float a bond to begin with when the extracted raw material had been generating significant amounts of cash for a long time and, if the remaining raw material was converted to a finished product, there should be more than enough cash to fund the diversification.

By my calculations, the asset's valuation didn't equate to the 40-year quad count over a wide range of crude prices. In fact, it appeared to be off by half. As I started to share my calculations around the office, I ran into what later turned out to be a well-choreographed cover-up of reserve manipulation and overstatement. The urgency to diversify was far greater than the public had been led to believe and the ruling family had intentionally been siphoning funds from the treasury to maintain the State's appearance of solvency and expected extravagance. All of my work products from the time of my initial inquiries were being called into question and I was asked to redo everything two to three times each. I was being intentionally tied off and distracted from probing this topic any more, at least while at work.

Fortunately, my flat mate was in the petrochemical industry with a specialty in geology. She was able to secure the underground sonic and radar mappings of the areas where the 40-year reserves of oil were supposed to be located. Best of all, she was able to read and interpret the mappings. Based on her analysis, the strata had sufficient gaps and pockets to hold the volume of oil required but the reflective density showed something other than oil. In fact, it showed something that would turn out to be far more valuable than oil. It was fresh water.

Normally, water wouldn't be more valuable than oil, but the recent surface water-based virus that was crisscrossing the globe did not permeate ground water. Apparently, something in the soil or rock strata immediately neutralized the virus. That meant water already underground represented the only potable water, and while the amounts underground were spread around the globe, large, documented pools did not exist, except of course, in my emirate.

It is estimated that the average person in a developed country used 80-100 gallons of water a day. Unlike oil, water is needed to sustain life. Having a large, documented pool of potable water represented a unique opportunity of potentially inestimable value. Given the water consumption stats, and the pool size, I came up with the following calculations:

Worldwide Population: 6 billion people

Average Daily Water Consumption (includes drinking, or personal consumption, plus other direct and indirect uses such as cleaning, irrigation for consumed food, etc.): 80 gallons/day/person

Daily Worldwide Consumption:

6,000,000,000 people × 80 gallons per person per day
= 480,000,000,000 gallons per day

Annual Worldwide Water Consumption:

480,000,000,000 gallons per day × 365 days per year
= 175,200,000,000,000 gallons per year

Volume holding 40 years + 80 years of emirate oil reserves:

1,300,000,000,000 gallons of oil used/year × 120 years =
156,000,000,000,000 gallons of capacity

156/175.2 = 0.89 years of the Worldwide
Water Requirement

Now, 89% of the annual worldwide water requirement might not seem like much, but the fact it was all in one place made it very unique. Determining its value, however, would be more difficult.

I started by creating the boundary conditions for my value calculation. Defining the low end would be easy. It is basically no or low value in an environment where water of this type was readily available everywhere and at no, or low, cost. On the other end of the spectrum is the assumption this was the only source of ground- based water in the world, meaning its value was priceless. Unfortunately, that broad of range was not helpful so I started tightening the conditions. On the low end, I assumed ground-based water was available in most locations but at a price that was sensitive to the availability of supply, the ability to produce and distribute, and its proximity to users. This sounded very familiar especially considering who I was working for! On the high end, I used the same parameters except I tightened the parameters of supply, production, distribution and proximity. Again, very familiar.

There was one thing, however, making this calculation different than my normal crude oil calculations. This resource, water, had the ability to be replenished via rain and the natural filtration effect of water moving through the soil and rock strata neutralizing the virus. Rainfall quantities, and the amount of time it takes for surface water to leach into underground sources, varies around the world, so to streamline the calculation a broad-based average would be required. Additionally, I could not ignore the obvious, namely the availability of sea water. It turned out that sea water did not carry the virus but also was not potable, so as a source it would require significant processing along with storage, distribution, and be subject to its proximity to consumers.

In the pre-virus environment, the average cost of bottled, naturally filtered, still drinking water was $0.06 per fluid ounce. With 128 ounces in a gallon, the per gallon cost would be $7.68. Then it occurred to me, the operative word was "drinking" water. My previous calculations were based upon total water consumption. The picture changes significantly if I were to split out the drinking water portion from the total. The recommended daily water consumption amount is 64 ounces, or one-half gallon. That equates to 183 gallons per year, so running that value back through my calculation says the emirate's underground water source equated to 142 years of drinking water. I was shocked. It was 22 years longer than the emirate's oil supply. And that's what made this the next big thing. The demand for oil would eventually dry up but that would never be the case for drinking water!

The Bunker

bunker: noun - a reinforced underground shelter, typically for use in wartime

The facility my team and I were assigned to audit was located about 50 miles northwest of downtown Houston, the U.S. seat of power for oil companies. The locals called it the bunker because it was built underground. The man who built and ran the facility was referred to as "James Bond" because of all his high-tech gadgetry and surveillance equipment.

To say the bunker was off the beaten path would be an understatement. We were so far out of the metropolitan area even grazing cattle were nowhere to be found. As we approached our destination, we passed through an electronic security gate in front of a nondescript metal-roofed building surrounded by dual 15-foot electrified fences. The building sat on the edge of a parking lot that looked to hold about 30 cars. Half of the spots were taken. Once we were inside the building, the only thing visible was the top of a concrete elevator shaft.

Without warning, a yellow-flashing light started up and tumblers could be heard moving into place as electronic locks on the doors we just came through were activated. A red light then flashed on the card reader near the elevator door. Once I swiped my magnetic identification card, the red light turned solid green and the door opened quickly. Upon entering the elevator car, we pushed the bottom button, "-5." The door finally closed and we started to descend.

When the door opened again, we found ourselves in a dark semi-circular room with floor-to-ceiling monitors consisting of video screens and old-school light boards outlining the nationwide natural gas pipeline distribution network. Most screens and lights glowed green or yellow with one small cluster of red lights centered near the Mississippi delta and the Gulf of Mexico. Workstations were facing away from the elevator door, so our arrival was signaled only by the sound of the elevator's door opening and the familiar ding from the arrival bell.

We were told the reason for this level of security was because in the wrong hands the nationwide natural gas pipeline could be turned into a multipoint Roman candle, causing simultaneous large-scale explosions and fires across the country. A 2010 incident in San Bruno, California was often cited as the example of what could happen, and because of that, our audit was focused on how to keep disasters like that from happening again.

The first step of this audit, like most, was to request documentation regarding all relevant business processes. From there, the team created an end-to-end operational flow which would subsequently be tested. Documentation demonstrating how the various business process steps are executed provided evidence of a process step either being followed or not. In my experience, this evidence can also show process gaps, areas of risk, lack of control and, ultimately, areas for improvement. Given the potential for disaster, however, process gaps here represent the potential for property destruction and death.

My audit team consisted of seven individuals plus myself. Three people were job content evaluation and process design experts. From the end-to-end operation flow, they would assess the skills of the people assigned to execute each step and validate how well they followed the process. Two team members were workflow and tool experts with experience managing the sources and sinks of data. They would be able to quickly identify issues with received information and the associated display and reporting mechanisms that alert the staff to issues and possible problems with the pipeline. Another team member was responsible for evaluating operational anomalies making sure exception reports were filed, tracked and resolved in the appropriate timeframes. The seventh and last member of the team was an expert in change management and communication. Her role was to evaluate the processes to provide notifications to local governmental agencies and the general public regarding problems with the pipeline.

Collectively, we were pleased with the level of detail in the process documents. The supporting materials evidencing proper execution of the process steps were equally impressive. This was simultaneously satisfying and disappointing, though, because as a function, we're basically paid to find and report on problems. In this case, however, we couldn't. On the morning of our onsite readout, just as we were packing up, an alarm horn went off in the main control room that was so loud and obnoxious we could hear it in our conference room. Since we had to walk back there in order to take the elevator to the surface, we were able to see firsthand what was going on. The light board outlining the nationwide natural gas pipeline was red from end to end. Half of the monitors were streaming television news feeds of fires burning from the cities home to each of the pipeline's terminal points. Apparently, someone had just executed a coordinated attack along the entire pipeline.

My team and I watched with interest as the control room staff shifted into crisis mode in order to stop the flow of natural gas. It was obvious to all of us their efforts weren't working. An announcement was then made in the room to commence secondary protocol, namely, to isolate sections of the pipeline. As that step played out, several of the red lights changed to yellow, but none turned green. We continued to watch with interest as the control room staff proceeded with their attempts to get back to green. From where we stood, the actions appeared well choreographed and seemed to go on for a long time. In actuality, we were only standing there three minutes.

Recognizing the seriousness of the situation, the team thought it was time to quietly leave, so we turned around and made our way to the elevator door at the back of the room. I swiped my magnetic identification card on the card reader to call the elevator; but unlike other times, the indicator light did not change to solid green. It continued to flash red. I repeated the process two more times, but nothing changed. After the last swipe, one of the staff members came up to us and said the facility was on lockdown, meaning no one could enter or exit. They further explained the facility was now operating on internal power and not connected to surface utilities, so we were basically in the equivalent of a missile silo during a nuclear attack. With that, we were asked to return to the conference room.

Over the next two hours, we watched with interest reports from the various news channels on the conference room television as well as the closed-circuit television feed from the control room. Several of the fires had already subsided with the isolation of the pipeline sections, and fire crews had gained control over the rest, so that part of the story was coming to an end. The real story regarding how this could happen, however, was just starting.

As we continued to sit in the conference room, I started to notice a flurry of footsteps and conversations coming our way but was unable to discern anything specific. Several times, the footsteps and conversations stopped right outside our conference room door, but no one came in. That was, until, someone did. It was "James Bond," the builder and general manager of the bunker. He had not been part of the audit we performed nor the read-out. In fact, up to this point we hadn't even seen him, but I'm sure he had known our every move. Unfortunately, the latter point is why he was now talking with us.

I listened incredulously to what was said as the implications for my team were hard to take in. It appears that one of the business process documents we had collected for the audit included a detailed description of how to conduct an attack on the pipeline for which there was no defense. It was this very type of attack that had just taken place.

The process document and attack description had been around for a very long time. It was no coincidence the attack took place during the time of our audit as someone on the team had leaked the information. The question regarding the leak was that no matter if it was intentional or unintentional, how could the information have gotten out? We weren't allowed to take any documents with us outside of the bunker, and because we were so far underground our mobile phones didn't work. The team did have secure internet and email access as part of the audit, so that had to be the transmission vehicle, but who was the point of origin?

I asked everyone to pull out their laptops, login to the network and open their Outlook Sent folders. Since we were all using a group "Send from" email, our Sent folders should all match exactly. I had everyone pass their computers to the person sitting to their left and we started to simultaneously scroll through the Sent items. 352 emails had been sent during the period of the audit and everyone's list matched. No spurious or errant emails had been sent so that left internet access as the culprit. While the devices we brought into the bunker were secured as part of the corporate network, it was possible to have malware introduced via an unsuspecting user clicking on a link or attachment they shouldn't. Additionally, the process documents we were given were all locally created by staff members in the bunker using either Word or Visio based upon homegrown templates and macros so they, too, could have some issues. To dig deeper, we were going to need an IT virus expert.

Because we were in lockdown mode, we wouldn't be able to have the company's IT virus expert join us in person, so the analysis process would be via remote diagnostic control on a laptop by laptop basis. This connection was easy to set up based upon everyone's IP address. In order to not appear to be targeting anyone specifically, we put our names into a bowl and drew names one by one. Coincidentally, my name was the first to be drawn, meaning my laptop would be first to undergo the diagnostic. After about 15 minutes of the remote scan, the phone in the conference room rang. It was the IT virus expert. My laptop was infected and the source of the information release, however, it was due to an undetected and well-hidden macro in the document itself. That meant it was of local origin from within the bunker itself. Someone in the facility had intentionally put in motion the events to release the information and had been waiting for the opportunity presented by our audit team's visit.

Since our audit was unannounced, it likely meant the document and macro had been lying in wait for some time. The document's change log indicated multiple owners and contributors over a period of several years so to know exactly where and when the macro first appeared would be difficult to determine unless previously archived versions were available for direct comparisons of size and content. Access to the archived versions, however, would only be possible with the approval of the bunker's general manager.

When we reached out to him for access approval, he wasn't surprised, and almost seemed to be expecting it. There was no evident reluctance to grant access and he turned quickly to his terminal to open the file directories for us. With that, the file and directory paths shifted from unhighlighted to highlighted text on our screens.

Back in the conference room, the team compared each archived version of the suspect process document to its preceding version and found the macro all the way back to Version 1. The author was the bunker's general manager. The initial version of the document had been created to justify the need for the bunker and to describe the risks associated with operating a gas pipeline across the country. The attack description had been included as a specific yet impossible scenario of what could happen and, despite it being indefensible, the scenario itself was never considered in the control or security mechanisms. Had the general manager intentionally puffed up the need for the bunker, or did he want to have something in place to prove the bunker's value? Or was it his built-in exit plan, escape valve or death wish?

We'll never know, because when we went back to his office he was nowhere to be found. In fact, the team spread out to look for him and he was nowhere to be found in the entire facility despite it being on lockdown. The single elevator to the surface never moved and the emergency escape stairwell doors had remained sealed. Since he had last been seen in his office, we went back there. On the center of his desk was a dog-eared book entitled *How To Disappear Completely and Never Be Found.*

Pocket Change

change: noun - coins as opposed to paper currency

I always carry a few coins in my pocket: a U.S.
penny, nickel, dime and quarter and a British one-pound
coin. Individually they have no significance nor amount to
much. I just like the way they sound as they rattle together
when I walk or jostle them. To the casual, and even the
trained, eye they appear to be just coins. But like most
things in my life they hold a secret, or I should say secrets.
You see, the nickel and the pound coin were given to me by
my employer on the same day I received my identification
badge and lanyard. My employer is the NSA, the National
Security Agency.

Unlike most of my fellow employees who are involved
in code breaking, electronic data collection and analysis, or
encryption, I am a data mule. I carry data to the NSA from
its worldwide sources the old-fashioned way, physically. I'm
basically the human data transport version of an air gapped
computer. Air gapping is a security measure that physically
isolates stored data and computers from unsecured networks
like the public internet or an unsecured local area network.

My division of the NSA is focused on global energy. I travel on an almost continuous basis by all means of transportation to all corners of the globe. It overwhelms me when I think of how far reaching my contacts, and ultimately the NSA's contacts, are. The coins in my pocket are used to carry and conceal information. When I started work, the data was provided on microfilm which then evolved to microdots. Today the data comes in the form of mini- or micro-SDHC cards. That means the quantity of data I can carry today is about 100 orders of magnitude more than when I started. Today, as in the past, the data goes inside the coins. The nickel can hold a micro-SDHC card and the pound coin can hold a mini-SDHC card. The trick is how to get them inside.

My most recent trip took me to Santo Domingo, Dominican Republic. As I always did, I stayed at the Jaragua Hotel & Casino. Most of the times I traveled there to call upon the local telephone company, Codetel. This frequent routine is what got me associated with the NSA to begin with. On this trip, however, as an NSA operative I was there to meet with an NSA contact from Venezuela. We both traveled and arrived separately under the guise of an island vacation. Our first meeting would be in the hotel at the Luna Bar, but the data transfer would actually take place at a local restaurant, El Meson de la Cava. This location was specifically selected because it was underground and not subject to electronic surveillance via satellite or adjacent buildings.

My favorite dish is also one of the restaurant's signature dishes, Tenderloin with Dijon Mustard Flambé. When served, it is flamed at the table which creates just enough attention and distraction to allow the SDHC cards to be handed off. They will be inserted into the coins once I'm back in my hotel room and, given all that had been going on in Venezuela recently, this data exchange was going to be critical. I was even instructed to return it directly to Fort Meade rather than use my normal dead drop. I could only imagine the information it might contain.

Upon entering the hotel, everything seemed to be normal, but when I got back to my room, I could tell someone else had been in there. The maid always did a nice job of placing slippers and a white linen floor mat at the side of the bed and arranging my toiletries and wash cloth in the bathroom in a very specific way. Both of these things were just enough out of position to indicate another person's touch, but who? It made me uncomfortable enough to pick up the phone and call my travel agent to arrange the next flight back to BWI which was an American flight at 8:05 a.m.

Needless to say, I didn't sleep much that night. I had my driver pick me up at the hotel at 5 a.m. for the 35-minute ride to the airport. There are two routes to the airport from the Jaragua; one follows the coast the whole way and goes through the Colonial Zone while the other swings inland to start but converges on the coastal route. We opted for the one through the Colonial Zone as it would be easier to see if a car was tailing us.

As we pulled out of the hotel, we were one of very few cars on the Malecon. That continued to be the case until we reached the area of the Naval Academy. Cars quickly surrounded us and effectively boxed us in. My driver tried to avoid the situation but couldn't. The lead car then proceeded to slow down and eventually stop. We were trapped. Two men got out of each of the four cars surrounding us and then made motions for us to also exit our vehicle. Without saying a word, they started going through everything in our car. My driver and I were also searched, and we had to empty our pockets and remove our wallets. The contents of everything we had were examined more closely than any search I had ever encountered before. Then, without saying a word, the eight men got back in their cars and drove off, leaving us with the task of gathering up all of our belongings. Nothing had been taken, not even the change we carried in our pockets.

Perhaps because it was still dark, or maybe because they looked so plain, none of the men noticed the ring I had on the middle finger of my left hand and the one I had on the ring finger of my right hand. It wouldn't have mattered, though, because their real purpose of being keys to locks hidden in plain sight would have never been figured out. After repacking the car, we started back to the airport and, without further incident, safely arrived at the terminal. Neither the driver nor I spoke about what had happened. He likely didn't think anything of it as it was not uncommon to have local police stop random cars for an occasional inspection or to issue a traffic ticket that could be "paid" on the spot. I, however, knew what they were looking for: the SDHC cards.

After passing through Immigration and paying the cash-only $20 departure tax, I proceeded towards airport security and their vintage metal detectors and x-ray machines. I put my suitcase and briefcase on the conveyor belt and placed the coins in my pocket into the plastic bowl on top of the x-ray machine for their usual visual inspection. After I walked through the metal detector and started to reach back and pick up the plastic bowl as I had done hundreds of times before, I noticed the security guard had placed it on the conveyor belt. I immediately felt my heart starting to beat faster. Would the x-rays give up the secret of the coins?

I watched with interest the expression of the x-ray operator as my suitcase and briefcase passed through the machine. The next thing through was going to be the plastic bowl of coins. About that time, the operator looked over at me picking up my bags and I smiled. By the time he looked back at his monitor, the bowl had already passed through and either the monitor didn't reveal anything, or they just didn't notice. I'll never know. I emptied the bowl's coins into my hand and dropped them back into my pocket.

Back at Fort Meade, I entered the data extraction secure room and promptly pulled out the nickel and pound coin, took off my rings and started the recovery of the SDHC cards. The process was actually quite simple if you knew what to do. The rings were notched to hold their respective size coins. By placing the coins face up in each ring, a hard tap of the ring to a firm surface would release the back of the coin from the front and expose its hidden contents. On cue, both coins opened and the two SDHC cards were now on the table. If that wasn't amazing enough, what happened next blew my mind. The leader of the Global Energy Directorate walked into the secure room and, picking up the cards, asked me to accompany her to her office.

Data mules were never taken anywhere inside the NSA complex. A data mule's entrance and exit from the secure room was via a private corridor connected directly to the outside. This was not only to protect the identity of the mule but to also help isolate the contents from the carrier. It is better, and safer, for a data mule to not know what they are carrying. Obviously, this was about to change. As she inserted the cards into her desktop terminal, two wall monitors lit up; one showed what appeared to be shipping manifests and equipment invoices and the other showed photos of what appeared to be underground and underwater pipelines. The letters on the paperwork and the markings on the pipes were Cyrillic script.

As she paged through the images on the two screens, I could hear her mumbling the words "yes" and "perfect." It was clear the contents helped her in some way, but I wasn't sure how. After about an hour of going through the images and reaching the last screen on each, she turned to me and asked if anyone knew I had these. I told her that someone must have suspected something based on my hotel room experience and the episode on the way to the Santo Domingo airport but that was it. She then picked up her phone and asked someone whose name I didn't recognize to join us in her office. About 30 seconds later, two armed security guards walked into the room and asked me to come with them. As the security guards and I left the office, I heard the words "You've done your country, and the worldwide energy industry, a great service."

It was only later that I learned what the contents of the SDHC cards contained while sitting in on a classified CIA briefing on natural resources. Venezuela never reports publicly on its reserves but the data I delivered showed a total of 300,878 metric tons of unprocessed oil and 161.2 tonnes of gold reserves. The oil data amounts to more than Iran, Iraq and Kuwait combined; the gold data amounts to more than South Africa, Nigeria and Ghana combined. Resources of that scale in such an unsuspecting location, and within such close proximity to the continental United States, poses as much of a threat as it does an opportunity. The question is: What to do about it?

Economic Hitman

hitman: noun - a person who is paid to kill someone, especially for a criminal or political organization

The contract of a lifetime had just been issued on the dark web for $50,000,000 and I was the recipient. It was the biggest objective ever conceived and would likely be nearly impossible to accomplish. As is always the case, I had no idea who issued the contract or where the money was going to come from. All I knew is that half of the contract's amount was already deposited to my numbered account in the Grand Caymans which meant I was on the hook. The size and complexity of the contract also meant I was about to embark upon something I had never been a part of before. So how exactly does one disrupt the United States oil industry?

I'm what's called an economic hitman. The concept and disruptive practice had been around for hundreds of years. The most recent and obvious example in the oil industry happened in the 1950s and the target then was the Iranian government under the Shah of Iran, Mohammad

Reza Pahlavi, also known as Mohammad Reza Shah. In order to make sure the Iranian production and flow of oil continued at the pace that consumption in the United States was demanding, the U.S. government enlisted economic hitmen to work inside Iran and with multinational oil companies to simultaneously build production and refinery infrastructure and influence the operations of the Iranian government to create a pro-U.S. and pro-multinational conglomerate political environment.

In the Iranian situation, the hitman's job was to kill resistance and remove roadblocks in the building of oil-related capabilities to promote the U.S. agenda, namely, access to an uninterrupted and increasing flow of crude oil. While you could argue the result was positive to the U.S. for a long period of time, the steps to accomplish the task, which were behind the scenes and in the shadows, were unseemly and mostly illegal. Because it was outside the U.S., and the specific actions taken were up to the hitmen themselves, there was no direct prosecutorial path back to anyone in the oil industry or Federal government. That doesn't make the actions moral or justifiable; it just makes them part of the cost of doing business in this industry.

Unlike the Iranian situation, which was to enable the flow of crude oil at the source, my contract was about disrupting the flow at the sink. As I always did with my economic hits, I started by whiteboarding the desired outcome and worked backwards to create a list of potential alternatives of how to accomplish the task. At this stage, I did not rule out any alternative but did stack rank them based upon speed, risk and plausibility. I also factored into the evaluation the amount of additional people and support required to execute each of them. This then would lead to a short list of three to five choices with the highest likelihood of success.

Since my contract was to be a disruptive action, the most logical approach was going to be to focus on choke points. In the case of petroleum, there were three major choke points: the inbound source of crude oil, the oil refinery, and the distribution network for refined products. The best choke point would also need to be of high economic value in order to inflict the most pain.

As with any hit, the action taken had to take place covertly but be publicly verifiable. Stopping the inbound flow of crude oil would be the easiest to accomplish simply based on the limited points of entry. Impacting an oil refinery's operation would be the most difficult and dangerous based on their locations, local security and the volatile nature of what they dealt with. Disrupting the distribution network would be the most geographically dispersed intervention requiring the most people, but it also was the least secure of the choke points and most vulnerable. It also had the highest economic value and would be the most publicly verifiable and visible spot to attack.

I started my scenario planning by creating a reverse logistics diagram of the retail supply chain. Working backwards from gasoline consumers at station pumps led me back to city hubs which then led back to the centralized distribution centers. Each of the major oil companies operated branded gas stations served by their own fleets of tanker trucks operating between all three points. The best point of aggregation for an impactful attack would be at the distribution centers serving city hubs. That also made the number of people I would need to include in the process the fewest required to impart the most harm. I also knew that there would be no way to cover all of the distribution centers countrywide, so I had to employ a mathematical model to calculate what locations to hit in order to have the desired disruptive impact.

I had taken a linear programming course back in my MBA days but only vaguely recalled the optimization techniques that would be required in this case, so it was time to hit the books. It had been previously determined that a 70% or more reduction of product at the pump would be enough to create an industry disruption. Converting that to a specific volume of gasoline, the corresponding number of tank trucks and ultimately the number of distribution centers involved would give me what I needed to know. Unfortunately, the density of distribution centers, their volume capabilities and the geographic spread of gas stations was not uniform. This was why I chose to employ the simplex method to identify the locations to hit.

The 15 locations identified by my model combined to make up the 70% objective. They are: Los Angeles, Long Beach, Elizabeth, Savannah, Seattle, Norfolk, Houston, Charleston, Oakland, Baltimore, Miami, Port Everglades, Jacksonville, Wilmington and Boston. The next question was who to deploy where and how to have them go about their task. For my team, I leveraged my contacts in the private sector and reached out to my explosive and demolition experts. Without telling them the specifics of what I wanted, the fact I was on the other end of the phone let them know what was going to be involved. This would be my Plan A. I also called my cyber-automation experts in order to have a viable and less physically destructive Plan B. Now it was a matter of deciding when to strike.

The contract for the hit did not give a specific date to take action; it only cited a "complete by" date. That date was 30 days out. Between now and then there were summer vacations, a national holiday, two air shows, a fleet week and a large outdoor concert on the half shell, not to mention multiple other types of water-based recreational outings at one or more of the 15 locations. In each case, a physically destructive event, while more dramatic, would cause collateral damage beyond just disrupting the oil industry. Based upon these factors, my Plan B became my Plan A.

I put the automation team on 48-hour notice in order to have them ready their cyberattack and had narrowed down the dates to three possible Tuesday mornings. The day of the week was important as it was the day for the major ingress and egress of gasoline. Disrupting one or both of the events would satisfy the contract and allow the remaining $25 million to be released to my Grand Cayman account. Obviously, this kept me very focused, but for the first time I had to admit I was a bit distracted.

I learned long ago not to question the motives behind the contracts I was assigned, and the source's anonymity kept me from being able to ask any questions or even draw any conclusions. Something as broad as "disrupt the United States' oil industry" triggered too many questions, however. At the top of the list of questions was "Who issued the contract and for what purpose?"

The "purpose" question could always be answered with something having to do with money, but this time it felt different, primarily because of the size of the contract. It was about five times larger than the average contract size issued over the last 10 years. The "who" list included everyone from pure environmentalists and alternative energy promoters to offshore oil producers and rogue governments. That combination of size and sources did not bode well for the parties involved in, or impacted by, the contract. It also didn't bode well for me or anyone else being able to successfully complete it and that was worrying me.

I had been involved with four other economic hits in my career and by all measures they were successful. The work was complex and dangerous, the risks were quantifiable, and the money was good. In each of those cases, multiple teams bid on the contracts and were awarded the work based on the pricing and completion date offered. This contract was a directed award targeting me and whatever group of people I would need to assist me. Could the contract itself be a setup to entrap me, or worse, to eliminate me?

The last Tuesday inside the 30-day window was finally upon us so I gave the cyber-automation experts the go-ahead to commence their work. The preparatory steps would take place 24 hours before the actual attack. They were mostly focused on accessing the network, breaking through firewalls and hacking account passwords to gain control over the valve systems that controlled the flow of gasoline. Without local valve control, deposits could not be accepted and withdrawals could not be made. This was the basis of our attack.

About twelve hours before initiating the shutdown, my cyber experts started to see a flurry of reverse network traces starting to take place, but they did not see evidence of a network shutdown or realignment of firewalls and passwords like a system administrator would normally do if they suspected an attack. This meant the administrator wasn't trying to block rogue access, but was trying to find out who had hacked their way in. In fact, the reverse trace was so fast, and originated from multiple simultaneous points, it was like a hack of its own, a distributed denial of service, or DDoS attack. It was almost as if they were expecting us. The force of the attack was so sophisticated that it was well beyond what the operators of the distribution centers could coordinate, or for that matter, what a normal corporate IT team could execute.

The DDoS attack ended as quickly as it started, but one thing was clear: it had completely disabled our ability to initiate the shutdown. On the surface, it didn't appear to deposit any virus software, but it disabled our computers' ethernet, Bluetooth and wireless network capabilities, but not before turning on the location services which we thought had been completely removed from our devices. That meant our location was now compromised and we needed to abort. The team, however, wanted to look for the digital fingerprint of who was on the other end of the attack before powering down their devices. This would take a little time but collectively we thought it was worth the risk. Unfortunately, no fingerprints were to be found and that says a lot considering the skills of my team. That fact, however, only led to one conclusion. The reverse trace originated from a governmental or intelligence agency.

As the team and I quickly packed up our improvised operations center, my mind was going over everything that had happened all the way back to the time the contract was awarded to me. From the size of the contract and it being a directed award, to the interval the contact had to be completed within, the conditions leading me to choose cyber versus explosive, and the objective itself, it was now clear I had been set up. The only question was by whom.

Over the years, through my business associates and successful contracts, I had developed several relationships with people in the Department of Energy and the CIA. While I couldn't ask a direct question, I could ask hypothetical or leading questions that bore resemblances to the $50,000,000 contract. And because it was now past the contract's expiration date, my interest was to identify the contract's sponsor and then see if I could figure out why I was targeted. I was looking for signs that my questions surprised people, struck a nerve, hit a little too close to home, or for indications of personal disappointment. My CIA contact was as cold as ice so either their training had kicked in or they really didn't know anything. My DoE contact, however, had several tells that indicated they heard or knew something. Rather than probe further on the topic of oil industry disruption, however, I shifted to questions regarding the Department's IT capabilities. They were more than happy to share details about the DoE's advanced IT resources, almost to the point of braggadocio.

As their story unfolded, it even crossed into the realm of being able to conduct a cyberattack like the one that hit my team. It was clear to me that the very group chartered to protect the U.S. supply of energy was the same one that issued the contract to disrupt the U.S. oil industry. And they were also the same one who stopped the disruption as a way to test their own protective measures. The contract's directed award to me was to ensure receipt by the team they thought had the best chance of being successful, and it was done on an entirely clandestine basis to make it as real as possible, all the way up to the point of potentially being successful. The $25,000,000 fee paid was a small amount to pay to verify the billion dollar-plus investment made by the DoE in IT infrastructure and staff could deal with a real-world situation an economic hitman could cause.

Three Lives

"*...everyone has three lives. Their public life, their private life, and their secret life.*" *Gabriel Garcia Marquez*

For most people, their three lives can be represented as three concentric circles of decreasing size with distinct borders as in the diagram below:

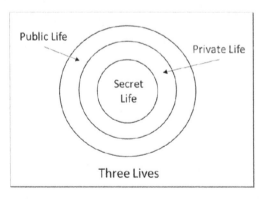

Three Lives

When items in the private life bleed over and become public, embarrassment can occur, and problems can ensue. The more the lines blur or disappear, the bigger the embarrassment or the larger a problem can become. Think of the situations many actors, actresses or politicians have faced in recent times. The recent college admissions scheme is a perfect example. The same is true for corporations, except the ramifications can be a bit more far reaching. Sexual misconduct and harassment can unseat business leaders quicker than poor results. When the secret life is breached, it can turn into a life or death situation.

Can an individual's or corporation's public, private and secret life ever be maintained so distinctly, or managed so separately, to avoid overlap or detection? The answer is yes, but to do so requires a lot of effort and consumes a lot of resources.

In my public life, I've relocated for job purposes multiple times. In my private life, I had just ended another relationship but dodged the marriage bullet this time. The one thing I had done differently than my counterparts was that I had kept my secret life so intertwined with my public and private life that I was basically hiding in plain sight. Using the guise of technology employers, professional associations, philanthropic activities and a myriad of business and personal trips that seemed to be very purposeful, I was able to move around the country and the world freely to meet with my contacts to both gather and disseminate information. That was my value. You see, I'm an isolator. I collect information and look for the unintended overlaps or connections between instances of the three lives in the global petroleum market and either mask or eliminate them.

Much like a preventor valve on an oil well, or an isolation circuit in a piece of electrical equipment, I keep things from connecting or flowing together when they shouldn't. I use the "six degrees of separation rule" and the "five whys method" to uncover connections and expose overlaps. These same tools help to make sure I'm isolated. For example, I've lived, worked and traveled everywhere in the U.S. except for one city, Houston. That's no coincidence as the physical office for my department was hidden in plain sight on the commodities floor of the Houston Street Exchange, the largest marketplace in the United States for crude oil of all types and refined products.

While you couldn't trace a finished product back to its original source, the characteristics of crude oil were distinct enough that you could. Whether by sulfur content, viscosity or the presence of other trace chemicals, enough was known about crude oil sources that an exact well source identification could be done with 95% accuracy. For the other 5%, you could at least determine a general geographic location. Mass spectrometry technology enabled both. Think of this as the oil industry's version of "23 And Me."

When the market started to experience a sudden and large influx of supply, I was asked to determine where it was coming from. After verifying this wasn't coming from the most likely sources, I was able to secure a sample of the unknown crude from Intertek Petroleum Laboratories. The mass spectrograph results showed a combination of markers that were previously unseen and not like any other crude that had ever been mapped. In fact, even the geographic details didn't line up with any known source locations. This was a new type of crude from a location that no one had tapped before.

Could this be a blend of several crude oils like the way wine makers blend multiple types of grapes to create a new varietal? Or was this truly a new type of crude from a location no one knew about? This had never happened before, or at least I had never seen or heard of it happening. Because of this situation, the board members of the Houston Street Exchange asked me to find the source. But where to start?

I went back to the Intertek lab to find out how they obtained their sample and from whom. The lab is required to keep detailed records of samples received by logging them in one by one using a specific date and time-stamped barcoding system that is cross-referenced to both provider and source location. This particular sample was marked with what appeared to be a valid date and time stamp, but the bar code did not register in the system. It was as if the sample appeared in the lab without going through the standard check-in process and was placed in the sequence of other samples to blend in. The placement, however, did give a rough indication as to when the sample was received; using that as a starting point, I went to the lab's security office to review videos.

After watching about seven hours of hallway and door videos, I finally came upon something interesting. There were three parties of two people each who came and went from the lab's drop-off point four times in the period of an hour. Their movements were synchronized to the point of being choreographed. Upon closer inspection, what appeared to only be drop-offs turned out to be a combination of drop-offs and pick-ups. The repetitive motion took the form of the classic shell game that you'd see a hustler run on a New York City street. This had to be how and when the unknown sample was delivered but from whom?

Wildcatters had always been a part of the oil industry. The name itself conjures up an image of frenetic activity, sniffing around randomly for something interesting, but not usually netting a result. In the case of the oil industry, it meant looking in places not normally known for having oil and it's that last part which offered the most likely explanation of what we had seen in the Intertek lab.

As an isolator, even I couldn't mask or hide the geographic markers in a sample of crude or refined oil, yet someone had either managed to do so or there's a previously unknown location of crude. But keep in mind, just because we couldn't identify the markers didn't mean they weren't there; we just didn't have them in our databases. So, for the first time, I was asked to isolate an isolator.

I started by mapping the unknown oil sample's characteristics to other samples in the database, looking for ones that were the most similar in hopes they would form sort of an "oil trail" to the source location. In the process of doing so, I also discovered a data pattern of my own, a fingerprint of sorts, to the producers of refined products. At the time I didn't think it would amount to anything important, but boy was I wrong. The oily fingerprint gave me a short list of producers who had at least either touched the unknown sample or whose refining processes were either used or directly copied in the production of the sample. This was the unknown sample's public life. By chasing down and eliminating all but one of the refiners, I was now on my way to discover the sample's private life. I monitored the tanker and pipeline deliveries of raw crude to them for several months, looking for any anomaly I could find in shipping manifests, volume measurements and even pipeline flow statistics. I even watched the telltale smokestacks and waste gas flames at several of their large refineries but didn't find anything unusual. I thought I was at a dead-end until I attended a training session about using the internet for remote monitoring and telemetry control of manufacturing processes where I had a revelation. I needed to get inside the actual data stream to see what couldn't be seen physically.

I hacked my way into the monitoring and telemetry Wi-Fi network to capture data, but without knowing the monitoring sources or receiving devices, the data was basically useless. Fortunately, at the high end of the market for extreme environments and reliability, there were only two possible monitoring devices, so I bought both. On the receiving end, both devices used the same data interface and analytical software to interpret the data, and since I had access to that software, I basically simulated the point-to-point connection from the real-world production environment and flowed the captured data into my parallel configuration. This told me that flow data was higher than what was being reported at the end of the process. It seems the data at the end of the process was being overwritten and made to look lower than it should have been. But where was that extra flow coming from?

To answer that question meant I'd have to check tanker ports and the Alaskan-Canadian oil pipeline. Since my public life had me in northern California, I started with the ports in Martinez. I used the guise of being a Control Systems Engineer and Inspector from the Division of Measurement Standards (DMS), part of the California Department of Food & Agriculture (CDFA). My electrical engineering background gave me just enough knowledge to fake my way through conversations with the onsite staff and my agency credentials looked intimidating enough that no one ever stared at them closely. They even gave me the ability to move around without an escort.

As I made my way through the facility, I was less interested in the mechanical aspects of flow and refining operations but really needed to see the various ship manifests and bills of lading associated with crude deliveries. The Control Platform office was the most likely location to find these documents, so I headed there first. Before a ship could off-load its crude through the facility's single buoy mooring and submarine pipeline, paperwork describing both the source and quantity of oil must be delivered to the Storage System Manager. This was to ensure sufficient onsite storage capacity was available and that the quality of crude would not contaminate either the facility or other deposits already onsite. I scanned the last three months' worth of crude deliveries and did not immediately see anything out of the ordinary for this location. The ships, their crude oil volumes and content were all consistent with the facility's normal processing operation.

Over the next three weeks, I would repeat this exercise at other West Coast and East Coast ports. Each time I would assume the identity of the corresponding state's measurements and standards bureau. I could find no anomalies. During my Mardi Gras trip to New Orleans, I took the opportunity to travel south and go to Port Fourchon in order to repeat my process there. Given this facility's capability to handle large volumes of crude oil and their pipeline connections to half of the U.S. refining capacity, including the refiner in question, the likelihood of this site being in play was high.

This time, I donned the persona of an inspector from the Pipeline Division of the Louisiana Department of Natural Resources. This allowed me to readily move between port and land-based pipelines. It made the facility inspection process easy, and I was also able to review the transport manifests showing who connected when, and what content they loaded into, and extracted from, the pipeline. Everything looked in order except for one thing: the output volumes exceeded the input volumes. That meant an unidentified source was being injected into the flow, but where and how?

Since flow is monitored at multiple points along a pipeline, it would be as simple as looking for a volume discontinuity between measurement points. Working backwards in this process, I traced the volume increase to one of the LOOP's three single buoy moorings and submarine pipelines. A tanker of unknown registry had been offloading their crude into the pipeline system. Their connection dates, times and volumes were not recorded by anyone and no one had noticed the flow and storage capacity anomalies. Even though I had previously determined the refiner, the producer was still eluding me, but with the use of LOOP, it must be from an offshore or international source. What I didn't know at the time, however, was this would turn out to be an incorrect assumption.

The flow discrepancies had started about four months before I received this assignment. During this period, volume fluctuations were occurring every three weeks, which meant it would be about time for another one to take place if the pattern continued. Since the single point moorings were just over 18 miles from shore and outside the territorial waters of the United States, I wouldn't be able to watch tanker traffic directly. I was going to need some other way to observe ship connections. My three choices were to bribe someone on the control platform, engage satellite surveillance, or to intercept webcam feeds.

Since the ship's connections hadn't been logged in the first place, it would be too risky to bribe someone onsite as they could be involved. Satellite repositioning to the Gulf would take too long and likely miss the connection window. This meant I had to again use my hacking skills, this time to intercept the webcam feeds. Fortunately, it was an easy task because no one thought the feeds were vulnerable being that far offshore.

After about two days of watching the video feeds, a mid-size tanker approached the terminal and proceeded to connect and discharge its load. This was unusual as this terminal was primarily used for super tankers given its deep-water location. Mid-size tankers were able to make their way closer to shore and use the coastal single point moorings. The markings on the ship were minimal but it was obvious the port of registry was in the United States and not of foreign origin. I was, however, able to get enough information about the ship to determine its transponder number and start tracking it via the GPS network. It headed south by southwest and finally dropped anchor in Texas City, Texas.

The Texas City location had multiple ports and companies involved with crude oil, refined petroleum products and natural gas, making it a perfect place to blend into the crowd. The "name brand" companies had already been ruled out during my oil sample analysis, so that meant figuring out how the unknown crude was entering the system. Since the only way to get crude onto a ship was via one of the two Marathon docks, I needed to infiltrate the Marathon storage tank system at the Port of Texas City.

For two months, I watched a constant stream of tanker trucks come and go; their tractors all indicated independent drivers and ICC MC numbers and registrations from Texas, Oklahoma and Iowa. Texas and Oklahoma made sense, but Iowa? There's no oil in Iowa, or at least that was the prevailing opinion. This would explain the lack of known geographic markers and the isolation of an unknown source. But how could it have remained hidden for so long and why did it just appear now? The answers to those questions were not mine to answer but I sure would like to meet the isolator that pulled it off!

The OIL Platform

platform: noun - a raised level surface on which people or things can stand

When most people hear the words "oil platform" their minds immediately go to the floating oil drilling rigs in the North Sea or Gulf of Mexico. While accurate, this wasn't the type of platform I was assigned to.

I'm part of the United States Space Force and my "oil platform" was actually the Orbiting Information Laboratory, or OIL. Assembled in just under six years on classified space shuttle flights starting with *Discovery* and STS-51-C on January 24, 1985 and concluding with *Atlantis* and STS-38 on November 15, 1990, the OIL Platform consisted of four satellites that came on-line during the seven flights. The combined scientific and military nature of the complete device was known only by a few people. The two capabilities were compartmented as were its operations.

I was assigned to the scientific functions and had no interaction with the people working on the military functions. In fact, we didn't even work in the same city. My daily routine included observation of active oil fields and producing locations as well as on facilities associated with the refining processes of crude oil. By tracking tanker, train and truck movements as well as monitoring the heat signatures associated with drilling and refining locations, estimates of production could be made. These are the leading indicators of the gasoline supply.

Most days the changes in movements and heat signatures were minimal, but today was different. All heat signatures were gone and all movements had stopped. At first, we thought our instruments had gone offline or failed. After running diagnostics and pointing OIL at our validation sites, we knew the equipment was operating correctly. When we focused again on the assigned locations, we saw the previous results. Nothing was happening. Per protocol, we reported the changes and absence of movement and heat signatures up the line. The reaction was almost instantaneous. Our location went into what must have been lockdown mode. The automatic fire doors shut; all window coverings were closed; the HVAC system shifted into internal recirculate mode and the overhead lighting changed over to a red glow. No one in the place had ever seen this happen before. We learned later that the facility changes we experienced also took place at the location responsible for OIL's military functions.

For those of us with live monitors the text on the screen which usually read DATA COLLECTION MODE changed into TARGETING MODE. We had never seen that happen before either. In fact, we weren't exactly sure what TARGETING MODE meant. On the wall-mounted master display which tracked the location of the four OIL satellites relative to the earth's rotation, we noticed their orbits starting to shift.

The normal alignment of OIL was based upon draft working documents that eventually became Patent US4854527 shortly after the STS-38 flight. This enabled the continuous and real-time observation of every location on the earth via a tetrahedral constellation of four satellites using elliptical orbits, two with perigees in one hemisphere and two with perigees in the other hemisphere, all following an orbital period of 27 hours. The new orbits appeared to be more of an equatorial orientation.

At the same time the orbits were changing on the master display, our normally highlighted observation locations and validation sites went dark and a completely different set of locations lit up. None of these new locations were labeled; however, it was easy to figure out what they were. We could identify country capital cities, population centers, transportation hubs and what could only be assumed to be military installations. What was more surprising to everyone in the room, however, was the inclusion of sites in the continental United States as well as all of the U.S. embassies, consulates and military bases around the world.

Around this same time, our Commanding Officer appeared on the floor and spoke to us through her headset. She said, "People, we have been placed on Red Alert indicating a Severe Risk of energy supply disruption. The last time we reached this level of alert was October 1973. As all of you know, this facility did not exist back then, so none of us have ever seen this alert status nor have we experienced what we're seeing happen now with the OIL Platform. Suffice it to say our sister facility handling OIL's military functions is fully operational and now in control. We will be asked to provide observational intelligence, so stay at your stations and await further orders." As she concluded her remarks and left the floor, we all just looked at each other and wondered what was going to happen next.

The next several hours were uneventful. The alert status remained red, targeting mode continued, and none of the usual heat signatures reappeared. As my twelve-hour shift came to an end, I expected all of us to be debriefed or at least talked to about what we saw. The only thing that happened was we were reminded of our security clearances and the non-disclosure agreements we had signed.

When I returned to work the next day, the facility was back in data collection mode, all of the expected heat signatures were back in place and the usual patterns of transportation were once again evident. During the shift change, there was no discussion of what had happened nor of when things returned to normal.

I later learned that things were different, however, at OIL's military installation. They were put into direct connection with the Pentagon's E ring and the White House Situation Room and given operational control of several key assets. For example, out of our eleven carrier strike groups, five were put into Condition III status, or Wartime Cruising, where one-third of the crew is on watch and strategic weapon stations are manned. Three of the five strike groups were also ordered to change course per their prime directive while the other two were already properly positioned. Since that status is monitored by the rest of the world's military forces, it triggered the corresponding elevation of their status. What was surprising, however, was that we were the only ones who knew the cause behind all of this.

As the weeks passed, the Commanding Officer was much more visible than she had been in the months preceding the Red Alert event. We were running daily diagnostics at each of our workstations and had weekly data protection drills. There was never a mention of the actual Red Alert event, however. Then, about two months later, we were all asked to come in sixty minutes prior to our shift. Upon arriving in the facility's Mess Hall, the Commanding Officer proceeded to give us an After Action briefing of the Red Alert. She started with an evaluation of our performance during the transition from data collection to targeting mode. The content then turned to the triggering event of the Red Alert, the loss of movement tracking and heat signatures. We had been hacked.

While the reality of what she just said started to sink in, the implications of what happened started to pour out. Most of the group started to think about the technology issues but several of us started to wonder who was behind it and why. With the right analysis of the technology, however, we'd be able to eliminate who wasn't responsible and, if we got lucky, may even be able to identify who was responsible. Of course, all of our minds immediately ran to, and wanted it to be, one of the classical bad actors: Russia, Libya, North Korea, China, Iraq, Cuba, Iran or Syria. Unfortunately, our biases had gotten the better of us and we totally forgot this was about oil. It also wasn't overtly military because the OIL Platform's true purpose was only known at the highest and most secure level of U.S. intelligence. So who would benefit most by the Platform's surveillance capabilities going offline? The answer was OPEC.

Having someone other than an OPEC member country aware of the workings of the organization posed a threat to the control they exerted over the petroleum industry and the global economy. The satellites could provide an early warning to a change in production and/or distribution intended to advantage OPEC member countries and disadvantage non-member countries. With the OIL Platform, non-member countries could proactively negate many of OPEC's actions. On a global scale, like the coverage provided by the OIL Platform, the loss of influence it represented to OPEC provided sufficient motive to effectuate the hack. The question of how the hack was done, however, was another matter.

The OIL Platform had three points of vulnerability: the OIL satellites doing the surveillance, their downlinks and the terrestrial installations. The satellites were not subject to hacking as they did not contain an uplink capable of accessing the operating system. The only uplink information that could accept information was in the navigational module and that had to do with positioning instructions. There wasn't even a physical input port to the operating system on the satellite should someone choose to intercept or capture it. The downlinks were susceptible if a signal source of sufficient power blocked the valid signal but that would require using the proper frequency, framing and synchronization to appear authentic. The signal would also have to utilize the same 1024-bit encryption key. So that left the terrestrial installations.

The military installation was off-limits to most people plus it was located deep inside one of the most secure military locations the U.S. operated, the Raven Rock Mountain Complex, or Site R. Being co-located with the Defense Threat Reduction Agency and considered the "underground Pentagon," the location was considered all but impenetrable. My installation, however, was more accessible and the most likely candidate for a hack. So this is where the investigation started.

After the assembly and before my shift started, I was asked to report to the main data center. Once there, I was ordered to physically inspect the server farm for misplugged cables and unlabeled connections. This task would end up taking me eight hours to complete. As tedious as it was, there were discernable patterns to the plug patterns of the cords as well as with the position of their labels. That allowed me to move relatively quickly up and down each row of equipment racks, at least until I got to this one cabinet. While the exterior blended into the rest of the row, the internal rack structure was loaded with equipment from a manufacturer I hadn't encountered before, MikroTik. I made a note of the equipment and its location but also observed its plug pattern and cable labeling were all in order so didn't think any more of it.

At the end of the shift when I reported on my physical inspection, I made a point of highlighting the MikroTik equipment. The Commanding Officer immediately asked me to take her to its location. We were accompanied by one of the Data Center Technicians, an MP and an FBI agent. When the cabinet was reopened, the Data Center Tech validated the cable configuration and labels and indicated they were all correct. The FBI agent asked the tech to get the serial number and date of manufacture from the equipment. Once the agent had the information, he validated the numbers on his phone and proceeded to tell the tech to start rerouting data away from the device and to isolate it from all traffic. All ten of its feeds were from the data collection and surveillance side of OIL's downlink receivers, and its outputs were primarily the monitoring room's computers which feed everyone's workstations, including mine. It turned out the MikroTik device was infected with the VPNFilter malware.

This malware was designed to steal data but also contained a "kill switch" that could disable the device on command. It was this "kill" function that caused our heat signatures and transportation sources to disappear. We had found the smoking gun, but still weren't sure how the trigger was pulled. Chasing that down was going to require a much deeper and personal level of investigation. I wasn't going to be able to participate in that step as I was going to be one of the people being looked at. My only hope was that my highlighting of the device would help me appear not guilty of pulling the trigger.

About the Author

Rick Butler was born in St. Louis, Missouri and has a B.A. in Physics from Saint Louis University and a B.S. in Electrical Engineering and an MBA from Washington University in St. Louis. He has lived and worked in cities across the United States, has lived and worked overseas twice, and has traveled to six of the seven continents at this point.

Being a long-time student of science and math, he has a propensity to recognize behavioral and economic patterns that extend over long periods of time. His inspiration comes from extensive travel, living abroad, and from seeing things that other people usually miss.

Rick has forged relationships with people in all walks of life and professionally is considered a subject matter expert in his current field, sales compensation. He has worked in high tech his entire career and excels in knitting together what to others might seem like disparate events. Getting to know Rick is like peeling an onion; there's a lot of layers. People who know and work with him are often surprised by his depth of knowledge in multiple areas along with the humor and creativity he brings to every situation. Rick has a story or personal experience for every situation that he explains away as just "knowing things." With all of the companies he has worked for, and all of the cities that he has lived in, there has to be more to him than meets the eye. People wonder, what else has he done or seen?